# THE
# SOCIETY

## "Until the truth is revealed, no one is safe"

by
Joy M. Pierre

ISBN: 979-8-9892642-1-6

Library of Congress Control Number: 2023915160

Editor: Joy M. Pierre and Gutemberg J. Pierre Sr.

Cover Design: Joy M. Pierre and Gutemberg J. Pierre Sr.

Printed in the United States of America.

# Table of Contents

# Chapter 1

Loud music filled the car as she danced holding the steering wheel with a tight grip and bouncing left to right. Despite it being a rainy night, her music still blasted, rattling the rearview mirror, while reminiscing about the date she just had. Two cars ahead she could see a black flatbed truck swerving.

It appeared as if someone was drinking so she slowed down to be clear of any destruction, but it didn't slow her down from having her own personal party while singing and bouncing. Looking through her rearview mirror, three vehicles back was a dark-colored SUV with tinted windows that she noticed leaving the restaurant at the same time she left. She looked down into the console of the car to get her cell phone, no phone.

Still driving, she reached into the backseat searching

around for her purse to dig, but no purse. She thought she knew exactly where it was, but she couldn't help but think if she had forgotten it in the restaurant. To make sure she didn't, she slowed the car down and lifted her butt from the seat to reach further into the backseat, seeing if it slid over or fell on the floor. The rain poured down heavily and her wiper blades were at their full maximum, still not allowing her to see the road. She tried focusing more on the road than her phone, but because the weather was bad, she needed it just in case of an emergency. Still needing to search, she slowed down more and pulled over to the shoulder of the road reaching further into the back seat. Still not seeing or feeling it. "Was she losing her mind?" With rain still beating again the car, she quickly turned forward hearing a loud bang on the driver window. It was a dark shadow beating it with their fist.

Startled, she shifted the gear into drive slamming on the gas pedal not managing to find her cell phone in time, so she screamed and panicked swerving to gain control of the car from the wet pavement. Not realizing she turned on a one-way street driving head-on with multiple cars until she saw bright headlights, slamming on the breaks. It was a gas station on the right side so she pulled in and threw the car in park. She sat there in silence for a few seconds. She yanked the door handle and swung open the car door, big drops of rain hit her. And then she jumped out of the car, slammed the door, and rushed to the entrance.

Making it in, she was soaking wet shaking the rain

from her shirt, feeling safe. While watching other customers enter and leave, she looked back at the car seeing
if anyone was behind her. From all the traffic entering
and leaving and the bright lights, she took a deep breath,
calming down looking up for the restroom sign.

There were multiple staff there stocking the shelves
and working the cash register. Teenagers were laughing loudly walking up and down aisles. There were also
truck drivers standing in the magazine aisle wearing
headphones, a pregnant lady, and a father holding his
toddler son's hand by the fountain drinks. She walked
to the bathroom, pushed the door open, and went in
looking herself in the mirror, trying to understand what
happened. She had no idea who it was beating on the
car window.

While walking toward the bathroom stall, she didn't
realize that someone walked in. Someone pushed her
from behind wearing a ski mask and forced her into
the stall. The both of them tussled loudly in the small
area. With barely any room heads were banged against
the stall wall and shoved into the door. She began gasping for air because of the tight grip of hands placed
around her neck.

Another person entered the bathroom while she
was being choked. The closer the footsteps approached
the tighter the hold was around her neck. On the urge
of passing out, the footsteps left the bathroom and she
managed to pry the hands from her neck and open the
stall trying to catch the attention of whomever it was

for help, but no one was in sight. She began coughing looking at the enemy who was tall, slim, and wearing a ski mask. There was no way she'd know who it was. They ran toward each other tussling again as she grabbed the enemy slamming them into the glass mirror on the wall with a burst of energy. Glass shattered.

The enemy gabbed their head shaking it from left to right, staggering backward. She knew she could win the fight now, by the looks of it. Her adrenaline kicked in as she ran toward them again, but the enemy moved out of the way and she ran up the wall, turned back kicking the opponent in the face, watching them fall to the ground.

She looked down at her hands in shock panicking, it was blood all over them. She didn't realize the tiny pieces of mirror left piercings on her skin. Being distracted by her bloody hands, the enemy gained strength, sneakily rising from the floor, slamming her face into the edge of the sink, knocking her unconscious, and running out of the bathroom leaving her lying on the floor in a pool of blood.

Minutes later the same footsteps entered the bathroom again. It was an employee who randomly checked the bathrooms to make sure they stayed clean at all times. Distracted whistling she didn't realize a body was on the floor until she looked down and saw a bloody mess. Not to mention, the floor was covered in blood that wasn't there minutes ago. She was in shock. Customers and staff heard a high-pitched scream and ran into the bathroom pushing her to the side. One employee

                                        Joy M Pierre

quickly ran and slid to the floor to check her pulse to see if she was alive, telling others to call 911 for help. Another was trying to clear the bathroom and get everyone out of the gas station for safety reasons. No one knew what happened and the security cameras were down on this day, which was odd.

After getting everyone out of the gas station, the police arrived ten minutes later. A store clerk rushed to open the door pointing them in the direction of the bathroom. An ambulance arrived, pulling out a gurney and rushing into the building. Detectives and flashing lights were everywhere. There were a ton of customers outside needing gas so the only way of paying for it would have been at the pumps.

Back inside the bathroom the Paramedics safely put the body on the gurney and rushed out. Janet was standing at the pump, pumping gas while she was being wheeled to the ambulance, and noticed her familiar red hair. She was very detail-oriented and never forgot a face, so she hung the pump and rushed over to see if it was who she thought it was. It was Samra.

Samra was her neighbor that lived next door that was only waved hello to when bypassing. Police officers pushed Janet back so she couldn't get too close. Janet stood there watching the scene for a while. Then she ran and jumped into her car, pulling off. There wasn't much Janet could do, but go to Samra's house and tell her husband. When she arrived, she threw the car in park and jumped out of the car running to the front door.  She hit the door with three loud knocks. The door swung open and she blurted Dallas's name and froze. It wasn't Dallas who opened the door, but it was his cousin, Mark. The two of them stared into each other eyes with anger. Flashing back, Janet thought of how he bumped into her at the grocery store, running the shopping cart into the back of her heel. This ended with a ton of yelling and food thrown. Mark didn't do it on purpose, he was digging into his pocket to get his cell phone when the cart hit her. After multiple attempts of trying to explain to Janet, she picked up a pack of ground beef and smacked him in the face with it. So, after staring at Mark for a while with the door open, Janet turned around and walked back to her car, getting in and slamming the car door, mad. She backed out of the driveway, and pulled into hers, speechless. It was weird that he opened the door and she had never seen him over there.

Hours later, Janet was at home drinking a soda and flipping through the channels on television. In shock, she stopped when she saw the gas station story, biting her straw. The news reporter told how there was an incident that happen in the bathroom and how a lady was found unconscious on the floor. It appeared that she was fighting with someone who could have been a male, because of how badly she was beaten. They also stated that the authorities weren't able to identify her, they're asking for anyone with information to call the crime hotline. Janet stood from the couch putting her soda on the table.

She rushed to the shoe rack, grabbing her shoes. She quickly slipped them on and began to tie them. She

                                    Joy M Pierre

paused for a few seconds, slowly taking them off and placing them back on the rack. She lowered her head as she walked back to the couch to sit. Going to the hospital wasn't a great idea. The past history with her psychiatrist left her incompetent on many levels. Janet picked up the pen and tapped it against the table in deep thought. This was her way of weighing her options about reality. After tapping her pen multiple times, she rushed to write down the hotline phone number and threw the pen against the table.

She laid back on the couch, closing her eyes thinking, if she could only get back to her psychiatrist's office, she could get her records. She sat there for moments contemplating on methods.

There was a knock at the front door. She sat there for a minute before getting up. With one hand on the door handle and the other turning the lock, she yanked open the door. In plain view, it was not who she expected it to be. It was Mark. She stared into his eyes for seconds and quickly tried slamming the door. He was on the other side pushing the door open with force. She placed her back against the door giving it one last push and shutting it close completely. Then she ran to the window to see if he was still there, but he was gone.

She ran past the couch to the coffee table to get the hotline number, staring at the television. She heard a loud shatter of glass. It came from the back of her house. Running toward the noise she saw broken glass on the kitchen floor and a brick. She ran back to the living room grabbed the telephone pressing one button for speed dial. Someone said hello, and then she blurted that it was happening again. She hung up the phone and ran up the stairs to grab her black duffle bag. Flying down a flight of stairs, she snatched her jacket, and shoes running out the front door.

She jumped in the car flooring the gas pedal to get to the hospital. She ran multiple red lights almost causing several accidents. When she made it to the hospital entrance, she drove past and turned into the staff parking lot, even though she wasn't an employee. First, she thought about how she needed to get to the 7th Floor to get her records from her psychiatrist, but that wasn't her only option.

Her psychiatrist not only worked at the hospital, but he had his own personal office too. So, she waited in her car in the same row, which was five cars away from his. After waiting for hours, she yawned four times and at the fifth yawn, she managed to doze off.

Her therapist came out of the hospital and walked in front of her car not realizing she was there sleeping. But, it was normal for employees to nap in their cars on breaks. Trying to unlock his car door, he accidentally pressed the lock button and his alarm sounded, startling Janet, awakening her. He threw his briefcase in the backseat and jumped into the car, speeding off in his black Mustang. He pulled off so fast that Janet hopped the parking lot curb in an attempt to catch up to him.

                                      Joy M Pierre

In a hurry, her therapist turned to get on the highway and pressed the gas pedal to the floor making it hard for Janet to keep up. So she bobbed and weaved through many cars to catch him. They had to be driving close to 100 mph. The therapist exited the highway and stopped at a local coffee shop. He opened the car door and was greeted by a lady in a pink polka-dot dress who hopped in and drove his car around the back of the coffee shop.

He stood outside the shop for seconds before entering. His table was properly set, so he walked over and took a seat by the window. It was a perfect spot for Janet to see everything from where she was parked. His waiter brought two coffee cups and two muffins to his table, Janet reached into her backseat, grabbed the baseball cap, and threw it on. She jumped out of the car, ran across the street to the coffee shop entrance, and opened the door. So no one saw her face, she lowered her head peeking in the direction of the therapist, and saw a man with his back turned wearing a red baseball cap getting ready to sit down with him at the table. This was the first time she learned her therapist possibly had another routine. It appeared that he had private sessions away from the hospital and his office. The guy in the red cap fist pounded the table and the cups and silverware rattled. Many customers looked in the direction of the noise to see what was happening. The man jumped up from his seat, slamming the cup on the table. The therapist bucked his eyes and placed his index finger on his lips, signaling him to calm down. He wasn't doing a great job because more attention was drawn to them.

A waitress walked back to their table and the guy jumped into her face pointing his finger. She jumped back as the therapist stood in front of her, but next, the guy rushed into his face, making him sit down. Everyone in the coffee shop was looking and the therapist lowered his head, embarrassed. Things weren't going the way he expected. The guy in the red cap sat back down and the therapist told him if he had one more outburst, their session would be over. He took it as a threat looking at the muffin, smacking it off the table watching it fly across the shop. The therapist froze because the session was getting out of hand. The guy stood up and walked off leaving him sitting at the table.

Surprised, the therapist jumped up going after him tugging on his arm and trying to get him to come back, but the guy in the red cap yanked his arm and threw up his fist, walking out the front door, frowning. The therapist went back to the table, gathering his things realizing that he didn't get a chance to write a new prescription for the guy, so trouble would soon be on the way.

Janet walked out of the shop to follow the guy in the red cap. She saw him walking toward parked cars, so she jogged to hers because she was curious about the conversation they had in the coffee shop. The guy jumped into a black SUV with silver trim. He quickly pulled off almost hitting a white van that pulled on the side of him. Loud horns were honked and tires squalled. He rolled down his window yelling at the other driver even though it wasn't the driver's fault. Janet was still trailing behind watching everything.

The guy in the red cap sped off again. Driving like a bat out of hell, he ignored stop signs and stop lights as if they never existed. Janet knew he would be pulled over after seeing how fast he flew past a police officer sitting in his cruiser on the side of the road. The guy had to be going about 60 Mph in a 35 Mph speed zone. Surprisingly the officer never moved because he was on his cell phone. Luckily not to get caught, the guy continued driving until he made it to a museum.

He stopped on the side of the building, jumped out, and ran to the trunk. He grabbed a crate, slid it close to him and grabbed a black ski mask with black shoes, and ran to the building. Janet began to think about why a ski mask was needed. It wasn't winter, a windy day, or Halloween. He pulled out a crowbar, broke the lock, and ran into the building. In a matter of seconds, the alarm sounded and he was still inside. Janet sat inside her car panicking, she didn't want to witness a burglary.

With him breaking into a high-security facility, she knew nothing good would come out of this. There were cameras everywhere. She also thought about how he would pull this off unless he was familiar with the museum's cameras. With Janet looking both ways wishing he would walk out, he didn't. She jumped out of the car and walked to the front of the building. There were two guards standing outside the front door talking and laughing, taking a break. They didn't hear the alarm.

The guards saw Janet approaching and one of them whose name was James whistled at her. The other guard

stopped her, asking her what she was doing in the neighborhood. Her excuse was, that she had been going to
new neighborhoods to site see. The guard that whistled
at her asked her on a date and she couldn't turn him
down knowing the guy with the red cap was in the museum potentially robbing it. Janet gave in and agreed to go
on a date with James. They exchanged phone numbers
and made plans to meet up later that week.

The guy with the red cap flew out of the building,
sprinting to his car. This time the guards heard a loud
boom and rushed to the side of the building where they
saw him jump into his vehicle and sped off.

One of the guards called the police and James ran
back to Janet to see if she was okay and yelling, "Get
across the street, the police are on the way." In no time,
the police surrounded the building, not allowing Janet
to leave. Janet was taken to the police department and
marked as an accomplice until she took a polygraph test.

As she sat in the examination room, a polygraph examiner named Mr. John, prepared to ask her a series of
questions to test her truthfulness.

Mr. John began by establishing a baseline for Janet's
physiological responses. He asked her a series of sim-
ple questions, such as her name and age, to which Janet
provided honest answers. These questions allowed the
examiner to establish a pattern of her truthful responses, which would serve as a reference point for the rest
of the test.

                                    Joy M Pierre

Once the baseline was established, Mr. John moved on to the related questions regarding the incident under investigation. He asked Janet about her involvement in the theft at the museum and her knowledge of the missing items. Janet maintained her innocence, intensely denying any involvement or knowledge of the theft.

Throughout the questioning, the polygraph machine recorded Janet's physiological responses, including changes in her heart rate, and blood pressure. The examiner closely monitored these responses, looking for significant changes that might indicate dishonesty.

As the test progressed, Janet remained calm and consistent in her responses. She maintained her innocence and appeared to be truthful according to the polygraph results.

Upon completing the questioning, Mr. John reviewed the polygraph charts and data. Considering Janet's consistent physiological responses and her solid denial of involvement, he determined that the results were inconclusive, anyway. Following the polygraph test, Janet was informed of the results and was told how the investigators would likely continue their investigation by continuing to view surveillance footage and evidence, and that she was free to go.

# Chapter 2

Over the next few days, Janet and James texted back and forth, getting to know each other better. They talked about their interests, their families, and their hopes for the future. Janet found herself looking forward to their date more and more with each passing day.

The day of the date arrived. Janet dressed carefully, choosing an outfit that made her feel confident and attractive. She arrived at the café early, feeling a little nervous but excited to see James again, but on a positive note.

As she waited for him to arrive, Janet looked around the café, taking in the sights and sounds of the busy atmosphere. Suddenly, she saw a familiar face across the room. It was James, but he wasn't wearing his guard uniform. Instead, he was dressed in a suit and tie, and he was sitting across from another woman, holding her hand and smiling at her with the same easy charm he had used on her.

Janet's heart sank as she realized what had happened. She had been fooled by a smooth-talking con artist, who had used his position as a guard to trick her into going on a date with him. She felt foolish and embarrassed, but also angry at James for playing with her emotions. As James looked up and saw Janet staring at him, his smile weakened for a moment. But then he quickly composed himself and stood up, walking over to where she was sitting.

With a smooth and confident voice, James said, "Hello Beautiful. Sorry, I'm late. I didn't mean to keep you waiting."

Janet wasn't interested in hearing his excuses. She stood up, grabbed her purse, and walked away without another word. As she walked away, she felt a sense of relief that she had seen through James' lies before things had gone any further. She also felt a twinge of disappointment that the romantic date she had been looking forward to had turned out to be nothing but a cruel hoax. She knew she should have followed her first mind when she wanted to hesitate about her date invitation. She knew it wasn't appropriate for a guard to ask her out, but she didn't want to make things awkward or uncomfortable. James was persistent, and he seemed genuinely interested in getting to know her better.

                                    JOY M PIERRE

Janet left the cafe, her heart racing with a mix of anger, and disappointment. She couldn't believe she had been fooled by James, the museum guard who had seemed so charming and genuine. She had let her guard down and allowed herself to be taken in by his flattery, never suspecting that he had a cruel sense of humor.

As she walked down the street, Janet's thoughts turned to the other woman she had seen James with at the café. She wondered who she was and what she knew about James' true identity. And how she could have been a victim too, lured in by his smooth talk and good looks.

Janet decided to investigate further. She walked back to the café and peeked in through the window, trying to get a better look at James and the other woman. She saw them laughing and chatting, seemingly oblivious to the fact that they had just played a cruel trick on her.

She felt a gush of anger at their coldness and decided to confront them, to let them know that they couldn't get away with treating people like this. So she marched into the café, her head held high and walked over to their table. James and the other woman looked up in surprise as she approached. Janet wasn't a conformational person but James pushed her this time.

"What the hell is going on here?" Janet demanded, her voice shaking with anger.

James' face darkened. "What do you mean?" he said in a defensive tone.

"You know damn well what I mean," Janet said. "You asked me out on a date, and then you show up here with another woman. Did you think this is funny? Did you think you could just play me like that?"

James' expression softened slightly. "Look, Janet, I'm sorry if I misled you. I just thought we had a connection, and I wanted to get to know you better. But I'm not a con artist or anything like that. This is just my sister."

Janet looked at the other woman, who was now studying her with a mixture of curiosity and concern. She realized that she had jumped to conclusions without knowing all the facts.

"I'm sorry," she said, lowering her anger. "I didn't mean to accuse you of anything. I guess I just got carried away."

James smiled and said. "It's okay, I understand, but can we still be friends?" Maybe we can take a walk in the museum together, without any expectations or anything like that."

Janet considered his offer. Despite her initial anger and disappointment, she still found herself drawn to James' charm and charisma. Maybe he wasn't such a bad guy after all.

"Sure," she said, smiling tentatively. "I'd like that." As they parted ways, James took a chance and leaned in to give Janet a gentle kiss on the cheek. Janet felt her heart flutter as she looked into his eyes, realizing that she was beginning to fall for him despite her earlier reservations.

Over the next week, they texted back and forth even more, getting to know each other better and sharing their interests and passions. James even surprised Janet with a bouquet of her favorite flowers at her workplace, earning a smile and a grateful hug.

On the day they met at the fancy museum, James took Janet on a guided tour of the exhibits, pointing out his favorite pieces and sharing interesting tidbits about each one. As they walked through the galleries, Janet couldn't help but notice the way James' eyes lit up when he talked about art, and the passion in his voice when he described the stories behind each piece.

As they came to a stop in front of a beautiful painting of a sunset over a peaceful lake, James turned to Janet and took her hand.

"Janet, I know we haven't known each other for very long, but I feel like we have a connection that's really special," he said with his voice low and intense. "I don't want to rush anything, but I just wanted to let you know that I really like you, and I hope that we can take things further between us."

Janet felt her heart jump in her chest as she looked up at James, her eyes watering with emotion.

"I feel the same way," she said, her voice barely above

a whisper. "I think there's something really special here, and I'm excited to see where it goes too."

James smiled and leaned in to kiss Janet gently on the lips, but she pulled away, hand in hand, looking him into his eyes.

As James and Janet continued to date, Janet became more and more charmed by James' easy attraction and adventurous spirit. They went on romantic walks in the park, attended concerts and art shows together, and even went on a weekend trip to the beach. Janet felt like she had finally found someone who understood and appreciated her for who she was.

But one night everything took a turn when Janet stumbled upon a news article online about a recent art theft at the museum where James worked. As she read through the details, she felt a chill run down her spine. It was a bold and brave heist, with a thief making off with several priceless paintings and sculptures.

Janet couldn't help but wonder if James knew anything about it. She tried to push the thought out of her mind, but it kept nagging at her. Finally, she decided to confront James about it.

"James, I need to ask you something," she said, her voice shaking slightly. "I know we never talked about this, but did you know anything about the art theft at the museum?"

James' expression hardened, and Janet could see a flicker of fear in his eyes.

"What are you talking about?" he said with a defensive voice.

"I saw an article online, and I couldn't help but wonder if you knew anything about it," Janet said in an accusing tone.

James sighed heavily, rubbing his eyes.

"Okay, look, Janet, I wasn't going to tell you this, but I do know who was behind the heist," he said with a serious and low voice. "It's someone I used to be friends with, but I had no idea he was planning something like this. I was shocked when I found out, and I didn't want anyone to know that I use to be a part of that crew."

Janet felt a surge of anger and betrayal contemplating on whether it what a good idea to be involved with him, or not. But she couldn't believe that James trusted her enough to tell her the truth about something risky like that and they just started dating. For all he knew she could have been an undercover cop.

"Why didn't you tell me before?" she said raising her voice. "Don't you trust me?"

James looked down at his feet, feeling hurt.

"It's not that. This is not just information you want

to pass around Janet. I knew you would judge me, and I couldn't bear the thought of hurting you and things are going so well."

Janet took a deep breath and looked into James' eyes, seeing the fear and vulnerability there. Despite her anger and disappointment, she still cared about him deeply.

"James, I'm not going to judge you," she said. "But you have to tell the authorities what you know. It's the right thing to do."

James nodded okay.

"I know," he said. "I'll do it. And I'll understand if you don't want to be bothered with me after this."

"I'm not going anywhere," Janet said, her voice firm. "You can count on me."

Despite James' promise to turn in his friend for the museum heist, he was caught off guard by an unexpected phone call.

"James, it's been a while," his friend said, in a smooth voice. "I hope you've been well."

James' stomach knotted as he recognized his friend's voice. He had no idea how to respond. "Man. What do you want?" James asked, with a tense voice.

"I have a job for us," his friend said in a lowering

                                    JOY M PIERRE

whisper. "Something big. And I know you have the skills to pull it off."

James' heart raced as he listened to his friend. The heist was risky, but the payoff was potentially enormous. And James couldn't help but feel the thrill of excitement of pulling off another successful job.

But then he thought of Janet, and the promise he had made to turn him in. He knew that he couldn't risk his future and his relationship with Janet for the sake of a quick payday.

"I can't do it," James said firmly. "I've moved on from that life, and I'm not going back."

There was a tense silence on the other end of the line, and James braced himself for his friend's response.

"You're making a mistake," his friend said finally. "But I understand. I'll have to find someone else to do the job."

James hung up the phone, his heart pounding with a mixture of fear and relief. He knew that he had made the right choice, but he also knew that his friend was not someone that took rejection lightly. He couldn't help but worry about what might happen next.

A few days had passed since James had declined his friend's offer for the heist, and he had started to feel a sense of relief that it was all over. He had spent most of his time with Janet, trying to forget about his past and focus on his future.

But one night he was walking Janet back to her apartment after dinner, he heard footsteps behind them. They both turned around but James told Janet to keep walking. He saw a shadowy figure approaching them, and his heart began to race.

"James," the figure said, and James recognized his friend's voice immediately. "We need to talk."

James could see the anger in his friend's eyes, and he knew that he was in trouble. But he continued walking, ignoring him.

Days later, James made it to work, stepping out of his car with a sense of caution. As soon as his foot hit the pavement, he noticed the same friend sprinting towards him with an urgency in his movements that confirmed a confrontation. He hoped that he could walk away from his past without any consequences, but he knew that his friend was not someone to take rejection lightly.

"Look, man, I told you I'm out," James said with a slightly shaking voice. "I can't risk going to jail. I'm a guard."

His friend stepped closer, their fists tightly clenched at their sides, their expression was a mixture of anger and frustration. The intensity in their voice sent a chill

                                          JOY M PIERRE

down James' spine, realizing that his hopes of escaping the consequences weren't over.

"You think you can just walk away from this? You owe me, James. And I always get what I'm owed."

"I know," James replied, his voice steady despite the uneasiness in his heart. "I can't deny the pain I've caused, and I won't make excuses for my actions. I know I owe you, and I'm ready to face the consequences."

His friend's jaw tightened, with a firm stare. It was clear that he wasn't going to let James off the hook easily. The fire in their eyes flickered with a desire for resolution, that justice be served for the emotional wounds inflicted upon them.

"You think words will make everything right?" his friend responded in a tone of bitterness. "Promises mean nothing unless they're backed by actions, James. You've caused damages that can't be erased with an apology."

James swallowed hard, understanding the weight of his friend's words. He had hoped for forgiveness, a chance to mend their fractured friendship, but he knew that earning back trust required more than ordinary words. It would demand a genuine commitment to change and a solid effort to correct the wrongs he had committed.

His friend's sudden outburst caught James off guard,

causing him to stumble backward as he charged toward him. He automatically raised his arms to defend himself, bracing for impact as they collided.

The force of the impact knocked James off balance, and the both of them struggled fiercely for a few tense moments. James could feel his friend's hands clamping onto him with his nails digging into his skin as he tried to overpower him. This wasn't an ordinary fight.

With a blast of adrenaline, James' strength pushed his friend away from him. After his burst of energy and catching his breath, he sprinted towards his car, with his heart pounding tremendously. He fumbled for his car keys, and his fingers tremble as he struggled to unlock the door. Behind him, he could hear his friend's foot-steps pounding against the pavement as he closed in on him. Just as he managed to unlock the door and jump into the driver's seat, his friend caught up to him, slamming his hands against the car window in rage, staring at James.

"You can't run from this, James!" he shouted, his voice filled with anger and frustration. "You owe me, and you're not getting away that easily!"

James gritted his teeth, his heart racing as he tried to compose himself. He knew that his friend was right. He couldn't simply run away from the consequences of his actions. But he also knew that engaging in a physical altercation would only worsen things.

Taking a deep breath, James' heart raced as his friend yanked him from the car with a sudden burst of aggression. Stumbling backward, his friend tried to regain his balance but fell onto the car parked next to him, triggering the alarm. When James realized he had the upper hand, another guard ran up.

"James, what's going on," with both of their hands tussling him to the ground.

"Please, calm down," the guard yelled with a stern tone looking at James trying to understand what the fight was about.

"James, call the police," turning the friend onto his stomach, placing his hands behind his back.

"Let's not get the law involved. Let me handle it," James said snapping back to his security guard mode.

The other guard looked up, squinting, staring into James' eyes to understand his choice. The other guard let the friend's arm go watching him jumped from the ground.

The friend said to James, "You think you can just make everything alright?" his friend's voice filled with a mix of anger and disappointment. "You've crossed a line, and you need to face the consequences. Stop being a baby."

James's mind raced, searching for a way to calm

the escalating tension. He realized that his words alone wouldn't be enough to calm his friend, and he needed to give the other guard some sort of explanation.

"I'm not asking you to forgive me right away," James said, his voice steady, despite the fear running through him. "But let's talk about this." There was a tense silence as his friend considered James' words. The anger was still there, but a spark of hope began to form.

In confusion the other guard tries to understand the conversation, "what is going on James," he asked, but James still ignored him.

Slowly, his friend took a step back, his face twisted with conflicting emotions. James watched as his friend turn to walk away with a mix of relief and nervousness. He knew that there was still a long road ahead, and rebuilding their friendship would require huge effort and understanding. But he was determined to face the consequences and work towards earning back the trust he had lost.

James was feeling the weight of his past mistakes bearing down on him. He knew that his friend was right, in a way. He did owe him for all the times he helped to keep him out of trouble in the past. But he also knew that he couldn't risk everything he had built with his new life.

"I can't do this," James yelled with his friend back turned, his voice barely above a whisper. "I have too

                                        JOY M PIERRE

much to lose."

His friend turned toward him and charged at him,
and James barely had time to react. The other guard
leaned against the trunk of the car parked next to James,
still looking. They struggled for a few moments, but with
a mix of fear and determination, James sprinted toward
his car door, his fingers trembling as he fumbled to jump
inside. Panicking and overwhelmed, he fought to regain
his composure and focused on starting the ignition.

As his friend chased him, James frantically started the engine and slammed the door shut, attempting
to roll off.

Breathing heavily, James glanced at his friend through
the car window, as he pulled out of the parking spot. His
friend's face was twisted with anger and frustration, his
fists clenched at his waist. The realization struck James
that he couldn't simply run away from the consequences
of his actions or the confusion within their friendship.

Taking a deep breath, James gathered his thoughts.
He knew he had to confront the situation head-on,
not just with the other guard, but with his friend, and
himself. Escaping in the car wouldn't solve anything;
it would only postpone things and deepen the wounds
between them.

James drove away anyway, his heart racing with
adrenaline, asking himself if he had made the right
choice. He couldn't get dragged back into a life of crime,

and he was determined to protect himself and his new
life. And because James' friend caught him off guard
he never made it to work that day, suspended from
the museum.

# Chapter 3

While James was busy working on getting his job back, Janet still tried to find ways to sneak into her psychiatrist's office to get her records, on her days off from work. She remained determined to get her hands on those precious records. She knew that her therapist had been keeping detailed notes on her sessions, and she desperately wanted to know what was written about her.

On the day James returned to work, Janet decided to make her move. She drove to the psychiatrist's office and waited until the staff had left for the day. Then, she slipped inside the building and made her way to his room. To her surprise, the door was unlocked. Janet cautiously stepped inside, trying to avoid making any noise, and tripping any alarms. She searched the room and finally found a file cabinet in the corner. She started to ransack the files, hoping to find her own.

As Janet rummaged through the files, her heart pounded in her chest. She knew her actions were risky and potentially illegal, but desperation pushed her forward. She was determined to find her file and uncover the secrets that were within.

After several minutes of searching, Janet's eyes landed on a file labeled "Janet Hampson." Her hands trembled as she pulled it out from the cabinet. Opening it, she skimmed through the pages, her eyes scanning the words, searching for answers. As she read through the notes, Janet's emotions became uncontrollable. She discovered observations made by the psychiatrist. The words were both comforting and alarming, as she realized the depth of her emotional and psychological disorder. But among the chaos of her emotions, Janet stumbled upon a piece of shocking information. There, on the last page of the file, was a handwritten note from the psychiatrist, changes made to the file contained falsified information, deliberately altering and misrepresenting her therapy sessions.

Janet's hands trembled even more, and anger coursed through her veins. She couldn't believe that her trust had been so unashamedly violated. It drove her determination to dig deeper, to uncover the truth that had been hidden. Janet carefully gathered the files related to her therapy sessions, ensuring not to leave any evidence of her intrusion behind. She knew that these documents held the key to revealing the extent of the dishonesty perpetrated by the psychiatrist.

Leaving the therapist's office, Janet slipped out of
the building, her mind racing with a mix of anger, frustration, and a newfound sense of purpose. She knew
that she had to carefully analyze the files and gather any
additional evidence to support her case.

Returning to her car, Janet sat in the driver's seat, the
files spread out before her. She examined each page, not-
ing disagreements, inconsistencies, and deliberate mis-
representations made by him. With each discovery, her
determination to expose the truth grew stronger. Realizing the gravity of the situation, Janet knew she couldn't
tackle this alone.

Over dinner, Janet's unease grew, and she knew she
couldn't continue keeping her secret from James any
longer. As they sat across from each other, the weight of
her actions were crashing down on her.

"James," Janet began, her voice filled with a mix of
guilt and vulnerability. "There's something important I
need to tell you."

James looked at her curiously, sensing the seriousness
in her tone. "What is it, Janet?" he asked, concern imprinted on his face.

Taking a deep breath, Janet gathered the courage to
confess. "Remember when I met you at the museum,
the day you were at work?" she started, her voice trem-

bling slightly.

"I have to admit that it wasn't a coincidence. I went there with the intention of finding out information. I followed the guy in the ski mask, but I didn't know he was robbing the museum. I just wanted to know what him and my therapist were talking about and why the two of them got into it. I know it's an excuse, but he has been writing bad things about me so I broke into his office and took my file."

"You did what Janet?" James blurted raising from his chair. Are you crazy, you could have been caught?"

Confusion filled James's eyes as he sat back down and leaned forward, his expression was a mixture of surprise and concern. "Janet, why would you do something like that?" he asked, his voice laced with worry.

Tears welled up in Janet's eyes as she struggled to find the right words. "I discovered that my therapist had falsified my therapy records," she admitted, her voice shaking with emotion. "I felt violated, and I needed to uncover the truth. But I know now that it was wrong."

Their dinner continued, with a renewed sense of honesty and openness. But James was still angry, thinking he knew who Janet was. "So what are you going to do with the files?" James muffled.

"I'm not sure, yet," she mumbled.

 

He had trusted Janet, and the fact that she had broken into her therapist's office made him question her decision and beliefs. He knew he had a previous life as a thief and what made it right for her to be one and not him. He continued to sit at the table even more disappointed that Janet had been hiding so much from him. They were supposed to be a team, and the fact that Janet had kept all of this a big secret from him made him feel like he could no longer trust her.

James walked to the bathroom, and Janet noticed a sudden change in his demeanor. She could sense that something was wrong, but didn't know what it was.

After a few minutes, James returned to the table and sat down next to Janet. He seemed distant and distracted as if his mind was somewhere else.

Janet tried making conversation with him, but James' mind was preoccupied. He excused himself from the table and went outside to make a phone call. Janet felt a sinking feeling in her stomach. She didn't know who James was talking to, but she had a bad feeling something was wrong. She tried to focus on the meal in front of her, but her mind was racing with questions and concerns. After what felt like an eternity, James returned to the table. He seemed calmer, but Janet could still sense the tension in the air.

"Is everything okay?" she asked.

James looked at her for a moment before responding. "I had to make a call, but everything's fine now," he insisted giving her the side eye.

Janet nodded, but she knew that things weren't really okay. As they continued eating, Janet tried to ignore her worries and focus on enjoying her time with him. But she couldn't shake the feeling that something wasn't right and that their relationship might never be the same again. They both stood from the table gave each other a hug and walked in opposite directions.

James became distant from Janet for protection, so he could stay focused. Over the next few weeks, James and his heist expert friend Brad continued to plan the elaborate heist that could potentially make millions of dollars. As James became increasingly focused on the heist, he spent countless hours going over every detail of the target. He became obsessed with the planning and preparation, studying the maps and blueprints of the building, the schedules of the security guards, and the habits of the people who worked there.

At times, James would stay up all night, going over the details of the heist and perfecting the plan. He barely slept and barely ate. He also knew that he had to keep up his appearances. So he continued to work, and spend time with friends, all while his mind was occupied with the details of the heist. He became increasingly para-noid, convinced that someone was onto him and that the heist was in danger of being stopped. The more James obsessed over the heist, the worse his thoughts became. When he did finally manage to fall asleep, he was overwhelmed by nightmares.

Like the dream he had when he saw the faces of the people, they robbed back in the day. And how they had a look of terror on their face. He could hear the screams and the cries for help, and he could feel the weight of the guilt and shame crashing down on him. His nightmares were so intense that James started to avoid sleep altogether. He would stay up late at night trying to distract himself with mindless activities, anything to keep himself from closing his eyes and reliving the horrors of the heist. James' irritable and moody behavior continued throughout the planning stages. He would snap at Brad whenever something wasn't going exactly as he wanted. Brad dragged James back into being a heist thief, so James knew to lash out at him pertaining to any concerns. He tried to talk to James about his behavior, but James just brushed him off. As the days grew closer to the heist he started to drink more, using alcohol to dull the pain and numb himself of the guilt.

Out of the blue Janet called to check on James and he asked her to come over. Janet could see James needed help. The house was a mess but Janet knew better. She could sense that something was off with James, and she couldn't shake the feeling that he was up to something dangerous. James left the house and went to the store to grab a few items for dinner.

Janet stumbled upon James' blueprints while cleaning his house, she felt a mix of curiosity and uneasiness. She knew that James had been acting strangely, and the blueprints seemed to confirm her suspicions that he was up to something shady.

At the same time, she didn't want to confront James about the blueprints. She didn't want him to know that she had found them, knowing it was a risk of damaging their trust again. Despite her concerns, she couldn't help but look through the blueprints in more detail.

As she examined his plans, she realized that they were for a heist. She felt a wave of panic come over her as if James was planning a robbery which meant he was putting himself in serious danger. She debated with herself over what to do, weighing the pros and cons of keeping the blueprints a secret versus revealing them to the authorities.

She decided to keep the blueprints hidden, but to keep a close eye on James and make sure he didn't get himself into too much trouble. She rationalized that she was doing the right thing by protecting James, but she couldn't shake the feeling that she was agreeing with whatever he was planning. She heard the sound of James' car pulling up outside. Panicking, she realized that she didn't have time to put the blueprints away before he came in.

In a split second, Janet grabbed the blueprints and hastily shoved them inside an armoire in the living room. She closed the door quickly and tried to act as normal as she normally did whenever James came around.

James immediately noticed that something was off. He had always been a bit of a neat freak, and he knew that his armoire was usually organized perfectly. As he looked at it, he could see that something was out of place.

"Janet, did you move something in there?" he asked in a suspicious tone.

Janet tried to play it cool. "No, of course not. Why would I move anything?"

James gave her a long, hard look, but ultimately decided to let it go. "Alright, nevermind then. I'm going to freshen up before dinner. Can you put the groceries away?"

As soon as he was out of sight, Janet rushed over to the armoire and opened it. She breathed a sigh of relief as she saw that the blueprints again. She quickly shoved them deeper into the back of the armoire, hoping that James wouldn't find them even if he did decide to look more closely.

Janet felt a sense of guilt and unease as she realized that she was keeping such a big secret from James. She knew that he was up to something shady, but she didn't have any concrete evidence to confront him with. She decided to keep a closer eye on him and to be more cautious about any other suspicious activities he did.

On a regular Janet went to James' house to clean.

One evening, as Janet was cleaning up after dinner, she heard James yelling from the other room. She couldn't make out what he was saying, but his voice was filled with rage and frustration. Janet hesitated for a moment, wondering whether she should intervene, but initially decided that it was better to stay out of it.

When James stormed into the kitchen a few minutes later, Janet could see that he was visibly upset. His face was flushed, and his hands were shaking with anger. Without saying a word, he stormed out of the house and slammed the door behind him.

As the door echoed shut, Janet felt a sense of relief wash over her. She knew that James' behavior was becoming increasingly unpredictable, and she was worried about what might happen if she continued to keep her secret.

Over the next few days, Janet tried to get James to open up to her about what he was planning. She would bring up the blueprints casually in conversations, hoping that he would offer some clue as to what he was up to. But every time she tried to mention the subject, James would shut down and become defensive. She tried to focus on her own life and work, but the weight of the secret hung over her like a dark cloud. And if James knew that she found those blueprints, he would be furious, and it would only make things worse.

She felt guilty for keeping James' blueprints a secret, but at the same time, she didn't want to betray his trust.

                                        JOY M PIERRE

She was caught in a difficult position but knew to keep things on a hush.

Regardless of her doubts, Janet knew that she needed to take action to prevent James from carrying out whatever plan he had in mind. She started some research on her own, to find out more about the blueprints and what they might be used for. She also reached out to some of her acquaintances in law enforcement, hoping to get some advice as well. But as Janet dug deeper into her investigation, she started to realize just how dangerous James' plan might be. She discovered that the blueprints were for a high-security facility like the museum where he worked and that James was planning to use them to carry out a heist. The more she learned, the more she had to keep quiet.

Janet's anxiety grew as she dug deeper into the details of James' plan. The blueprints were for a facility with state-of-the-art security systems, making any attempt to break into an incredibly risky plan. She knew that James could have potentially been a thief, and it would be difficult to make it through the high tech infrared motion sensor at the facility. She couldn't stand by and watch as James put himself in harm's way. She needed to find a way to stop him before it was too late.

She decided to confront him, hoping to deter him from going through with his plan. She arranged to meet him at a local coffee shop. Sitting at the table she took a deep breath and mentioned the subject.

"James, I know what you're planning," she said, her voice trembling slightly.

James looked at her, his eyes narrowing in suspicion. "What are you talking about?"

"The blueprints, James. I found them in your house," she said raising her voice. "I know you're planning a heist."

James' face hardened, and Janet could see the anger building in his eyes.

"You had no right to go through my things, Janet."

"I didn't go through your things," she said. "I stumbled upon them accidentally. But that's not the point, James. You can't go through with this. It's too dangerous."

James stared at her for a long moment, he stood up with his face unreadable. "You don't know what you're talking about," he said finally in a low voice, walking away from the table.

Janet could see that her words were pointless and had no effect on him. James was determined to carry out his plan, no matter the cost. She felt a wave of helplessness come over her as she realized that she might be the only obstacle standing between him and a disaster.

One evening, Janet received a call from James. He

                                    JOY M PIERRE

wanted to meet with her again, possibly to apologize for walking out on her the last time. But Janet could tell from his tone that he was agitated. James wanted to meet at a park near his place. When they met, Janet could see the anxiety imprinted on his face. "Janet, I need your help," he said. "Something's gone wrong with the plan. I don't know what to do."

"What are you talking about?" she said "I hope you're not trying to do anything stupid. Does this have something to do with the blueprints?"

Taking a deep breath and sighing he said, "Yes I'm talking about the blueprints. The ones you claim you stumbled upon," James mumbled.

Janet's heart sank. She had been hoping that James would change his mind, but it seemed that he was determined to go through with the heist, anyway.

"What happened?" Janet asked.

"I don't know," James said, his voice growing more frantic. "One of the alarms went off today, and the security guards are on high alert. I can't get in without being detected."

Janet thought quickly. "Okay, so the last time I wanted to talk to you about this, you brushed me off. Now you want my help?" giving James the side eye.

"Janet, I don't have time for this I really need you,

and you are the only one I trust with this information," James said in a slow mumbling tone.

"So if I help you, what's in it for me?" Janet asked while biting her lip.

James raised his voice, "I can't make any promises right now, but believe me I will take care of you when the time is right."

Okay so, we need to regroup and come up with a new plan," she said with her mind racing. "Let's go back to your place and figure this out."

They rushed back to James' house, and Janet immediately got to work. She ran to the armoire and snatched out the blueprints and studied them, looking for a way to bypass the security systems and get into the facility undetected. James was shocked that she knew exactly where the blueprints were. But he never said a word because he needed her.

After hours of analyzing the plans, she finally found a weak spot in the surveillance system that they could manipulate. And she also saw a photo of someone familiar with the word Leader attached to the bottom, but couldn't understand why James had the photo paper clipped to the blueprint. Janet thought she looked over the entire blueprint the first time, but when she heard James pulling up, she rushed to stash it away, and not realizing there was more attached to it.

                    

So she turned toward James, "Okay, here's what we're going to do," she said, outlining her plan to James. "We're going to enter through the side entrance and make our way to the main exhibit hall. We'll disable the cameras and bypass the motion detectors, and then we'll have a clear path to the target."

James looked at her, his eyes wide, and said, "You are not going with me. And are you sure this will work?" Janet nodded. "Are you serious? I'm not going and I'm helping you, so you won't be caught. Well fine, it's your best shot. You have to move fast, though. You won't have much time."

Janet's anger burned within her, intensifying into a raging fury directed at James. She couldn't believe that someone who was supposed to be so knowledgeable let her down so harshly. Her expectations shattered, and resentment flowed through her veins.

In her mind, she had seen James as the one who could guide her, mentor her, and provide the opportunities she needed. Yet, he had denied her the chance to participate, dismissing her without considering her potential. The unfairness of his actions fueled her anger, pushing her to a breaking point.

Unable to contain her frustration any longer, Janet turned her back on James, cutting ties and walking away. She had no desire to be associated with someone who didn't value her abilities or respect her ambitions. The disappointment ran deep, leaving scars that would take time to heal if they ever did.

As she distanced herself from James, a mix of sadness and anger flowed through Janet. She had placed her hopes and desires in his hands, only to be rejected and invalidated. It felt like a betrayal, a crushing blow to her self-confidence and trust in others.

# Chapter 4

Boom, boom, boom. James heard a loud pounding at his front door, it was his sister Carrie who was at the coffee shop with him that day he planned a date with Janet. While James yanked the door open, she fell in, hysterical.

"James it's Samra, she was beaten in the bathroom at a gas station."

"Where is she now," James yelled grabbing his shoes and jacket.

"She's at the hospital," Carrie said while rubbing her forehead and looking away from James.

It's been three months and they were just finding out that she was hospitalized. Samra was the type that only reached out to her brother and sister on special occasions like holidays, birthdays, or emergencies.

James rushed out of the door without another word, his mind racing with thoughts about Samra. He couldn't believe that his sister had been beaten and had been in the hospital that long without them knowing. He felt guilty for not keeping in touch with her more often. As he drove to the hospital, James called Janet, but the phone just rang and rang.

Making it to the hospital, James ran to the front desk to see which room Samra occupied. Entering the room, a wave of shock and sadness washed over him as he saw his sister, Samra, lying in the hospital bed. Her face with visible marks of the torment she had endured, with bruises and cuts telling a story of pain and suffering. It was bottomless to him that someone could inflict so much harm on his much loved sister.

Gently, he approached the bed, his heart heavy with a mixture of emotions. Taking her hand in his, he could feel the warmth of her touch, a flicker of life that gave him hope within the darkness of the situation. His voice trembled with both pain and tenderness as he began to loudly yell her name.

"Samra," he shouted, his voice filled with love and concern. "It's me, James. I'm here with you. You're not alone."

Tears welled up in James' eyes as he imagined the

 

pain Samra had endured during her three-month coma, unaware of the world around her. He couldn't imagine the suffering she had gone through or the strength she gathered to survive. But now that she had awakened, he was determined to be her support, and her shelter in the storm.

In that hospital room, amongst the beeping of machines and the scent of antiseptic, James held onto hope, wishing her memory come back completely. And as he continued to talk to Samra, his voice filled with solid faith, he knew that their bond would be the guiding light that led them through the long road to recovery, and to help identify the perpetrator.

Over the next few days, James and his sister Carrie learned more about what had happened to Samra. She had been alone and had stopped at a gas station to use the bathroom when she was attacked by someone who could possibly be a man, with a black ski mask. She had been left for dead in the bathroom, but luckily someone had found her and called the police.

As Samra slowly started to recover, James and Carrie visited her in the hospital every day. They brought her flowers, food, and anything else she needed. James even took time off from work at the museum to stay with her and help her in any way he could, and to make sure she was protected inside the hospital.

As James focused on helping Samra recover, his absence from the heist crew didn't go unnoticed. His fellow thieves were growing increasingly impatient, and some even began to question his loyalty to the team.

One day, as James was leaving the hospital after visiting Samra, he received a call from his crew leader.

"James, where have you been?" the leader asked. "We need you back. The date is coming up soon, and you need to be here to make sure you understand the plans."

James hesitated. He knew Samra needed his help, but he also felt a sense of obligation to his crew. "My bad, but I can't come back right now," he said. "I have to take care of something first."

The crew leader sighed. "Okay, but you are taking too long. And the job can't be done without you."

As James hung up the phone, he couldn't help but feel conflicted. He didn't want to let the crew down, but he also didn't want to abandon his sister when she needed him the most.

Over the next few days, James tried to balance his responsibilities to both his sister and his crew. He would spend the mornings in the hospital with Samra, taking her to physical therapy and helping her with her recovery. In the afternoons, he would meet with his crew, going over more plans for the heist.

As the days ticked by and got closer to the heist, James' stress and anxiety over barred him more. The

                                    JOY M PIERRE

weight of the operation pressed heavily on his shoulders, consuming his thoughts and bottling his energy. Every waking moment away from his sister was filled with careful planning, coordinating with his crew, and ensuring that every detail of the heist was accounted for. The constant juggling of responsibilities and the weight of the potential consequences wore him down, physically and mentally.

Despite his best efforts to maintain focus, James found his mind wandering, unable to concentrate for extended periods. He would often catch himself lost in a fog of fatigue, struggling to retain crucial information or make sound decisions. The feeling of exhaustion had taken over, leaving him shaky on the edge of a physical and emotional breakdown.

One evening after an exhausting meeting with his crew, James left on the journey to his home. His eyelids felt heavy, and his mind yearned for relief. Fatigue leached through his bones, clouding his judgment as he fought to stay awake behind the wheel. In the midst of battling his drowsiness, a quick lapse in concentration occurred. James' eyes drooped shut, his hands slipped from the wheel, and his car veered off course. In an instant, the screeching sound of tires skidding met the crunching of metal as his vehicle collided with an immovable object.

The impact shook James awake, his heart pounding in his chest as he took in the scene of the accident. The wreckage of his car surrounded him, a stark reminder of the dangers of his current state. It was a wake-up call, both symbolically and literally, forcing him to confront the consequences of his ruthless pursuit of the heist. The accident became a symbol of his own vulnerability, a reminder that he couldn't continue down this path without tending to his own well-being.

As James realized he was in a wreck, shaken but physically unharmed, he realized the gravity of the situation. It was clear that he had reached his breaking point, his body and mind unable to withstand the relentless strain he had subjected himself to.

But, because James wasn't seriously injured, he understood that he couldn't continue to balance both his sister and his criminal activities. He had to make a choice.

So, the next day, James called his crew leader and told him that he was out. "I can't do this anymore," he said.

The crew leader was furious and threatened James, saying that he couldn't just quit and expect to walk away without any consequences. James knew that he was taking a risk from his choices. Over the next few weeks, James kept a low profile and avoided contact with his former crew members, keeping his stress level down.

On another day, as James was out running errands, he received a call from an unknown number. He hesitated before answering, unsure of who might be on the other end.

                    

"James, it's me," said the voice on the other end of the line. It was his crew leader. "We need you back. We have a new work load after this one is over." James shook his head. "I told you, I'm out. I don't want this life."

The leader sighed. "You don't have a choice, James. You know what will happen if you don't come back."

James felt a knot form inside his stomach. He knew that his leader wasn't bluffing. If he didn't go back to the crew, he felt they would go after his family.

"I need some time to think about it," he said, trying to buy himself some time.

"Fine, but you don't have long," the crew leader replied before hanging up.

For the next few days, James was on edge. He couldn't concentrate on anything and was constantly looking over his shoulder, afraid that his crew was watching him. One evening, as he was sitting at home, he heard a loud knock on the door. James' heart skipped a beat as he saw Henry standing on the other side of the door, through the peephole. All James remembers was the fight they had in the museum's parking lot. James' mind raced with thoughts of betrayal and danger because of the confrontation that happen between them. He hesitated for a moment, unsure of what to expect, knowing he could be there to finish the fight.

After a few deep breaths, James decided to open
the door, with caution. James stepped back in defensive
mode, but Henry stepped inside, his face filled with
worry and firmness. James could see the anxiety in his
friend's eyes and knew that something serious must have
brought him there.

"What's going on, Henry?" James asked, his voice
filled with a mix of concern and suspicion. "Why
are you here?"

Henry's hands trembled slightly as he spoke. "James,
I know we've had our differences in the past, but I need
your help Man. I've been living in fear ever since our last
job together. There are whispers of revenge, and I think
they're coming after us."

James's paranoia surged as he listened to
Henry's words.

"Henry, what do you mean?" James did feel a sense
of awkwardness ever since the mission was complete,
but he didn't take it serious to think if someone was
watching him, or waiting for the right moment to strike.
The possibility of someone coming after him for revenge was shaky.

"Are you certain, Henry? I mean, I sort of felt someone following me the other day, but nothing serious.
How do you know we're being targeted?" James asked
his voice with a bit of suspicion.

                                JOY M PIERRE

Henry took a deep breath, his eyes scanning the room. Henry told how he had been following Samra that rainy night she was beaten in the bathroom. James frown, fist tight at his waist.

"It wasn't me James, I promise. It was him. All of it was for him. The leader paid a criminal to follow Samra and scare her."

Henry had gone along with it, thinking it was just another job, but he had quickly realized that he had made a terrible mistake when the criminal beat Samra up. Henry had tried to speak up sooner, but the criminal had threatened him and his family.

Henry blurted, "I went into hiding, because I knew that the criminals were looking for me, and I had nowhere else to turn. I've been receiving anonymous threats by calls. And they mentioned both of our names at times, James. They know we wanted out."

James's mind raced, replaying memories of their past actions and the enemies they had made. "We can't stay here," James said firmly. "We need to gather a team, ones we trust, and find a safe place. We have to stay one step ahead of them."

Henry nodded, his expression reflecting a mixture of fear and determination. They both knew that time would crunch down on them, so they had to act fast and be careful to protect themselves.

They found a secretive hotel that night, James and Henry worked diligently, reaching out to their trusted buddies from their past lives. They gathered a small group of skilled individuals who were willing to stand by as lookouts. Together, they developed a plan to go back to their once before secret location for members only. The location was only for those who had an anchor tattoo. And both James and Henry carried one on their upper bicep, allowing them a free pass in.

Being in this environment, you live by a code of ethics set for the members of the organization. So, anyone who violates the code can result in being sanction, including termination.

Over the next few days, James and Henry gathered more information about the guy in the black ski mask and their leader's organization. But, because James knew where to find the leader, finding the attacker was no problem. He knew that his leader's organization was powerful and well-armed, but James was known for his thorough planning and attention to detail. Without needing to buy weapons, James' room had a secret cabinet. There were guns, knives, brass knuckles, ropes, handcuffs, Tasers, state-of-the-art surveillance equipment, and lock-picking tools.

James knew that having the right gear could make all the difference between life and death. He also made sure that they knew exactly what to do and that they had trained extensively for the operation.

After days of careful planning and preparation led James and Henry to a critical moment as they quietly entered the door that granted them access to the heart of the leader's organization. Adrenaline flowed through James' veins, his heart pounding in his chest, as he took cautious steps down the dimly lit hallway. Every footfall was deliberate, every breath measured, as he and Henry navigated through the double-crossing domain of their enemy. As they approached the end of the hall, tension hung heavy in the air. James could feel the weight of the confrontation approaching before him, his eyes fixed on the figure of the leader standing at the far end of the room. There was silence, broken only by the faint hum of electricity and the sound of their own breathing. Time was standing still as James and the leader locked eyes, each aware of the significance of this moment. The intensity in the room was deep as they silently measured each other, a battle of wills playing out in their unspoken communication.

In a matter of seconds, James felt a gush of con-flicting emotions. There was fear, for the leader held an enormous amount of power and influence within the organization. The silence stretched, the weight of their stares holding the room in suspense. Both James and the leader knew that this encounter could determine the fate of their destinies. It was a battle fought with eyes and the weight of unspoken words, a clash of determination and boldness.

Finally, the leader broke the silence, his voice drip-ping with a mix of authority and curiosity. "James," he said, his tone a blend of respect and caution. "You've come a long way to face me. What are you doing here?"

James held his ground, his stare was steady. "Don't question me. You know why I'm here," he replied, his voice firm and strong. "You went after my sister and the word is, you're after me."

The crew leader's expression flickered, a brief glimpse of surprise crossing his features. He didn't expect James to be so tough but obedient and submissive. He was wronged by James' actions, an example of boldness and strength. And James was not punking out. For a moment, the room hung in a mild balance with thick air. The crew leader's next move could alter the course of their confrontation, sparking a violent clash. As seconds stretched into eternity, James braced himself for whatever laid ahead, ready to face the consequences of his actions another way. The room remained frozen, but filled with anticipation of a brawl.

"I'm not taking no more of this," James yelled with determination.

The crew leader smirked, a twisted smile rubbing his chin. "You must have forgotten who trained you, James. You can't stop me. You're nothing, James. You are just a minimal-waged museum guard. I've tried helping you, but all you gave me were excuses."

Without warning, the crew leader flew from behind the desk and attacked James, making him fall to

　　　　　　　　JOY M PIERRE

the ground. The leader saddled James on the ground, aiming a punch at his face. James dodges the blow, his training and reflexes kicking in. He reacted, throwing the crew leader off of him, with a swift response. With both of them standing, James strikes the crew leader in the stomach with a kick, mono a mono style. The crew leader staggered but quickly regained his composure, throwing multiple punches and kicks with deadly force. The standoff between James and his crew leader turned into a brutal fight, their bodies continued trading blows, each fueled by violent willpower to win victoriously. It was a battle of strength, skill, and pure ambition. Despite the pain flowing through his battered body, James fought on, his mind focused on the mission, thinking about what happened to Samra, not wanting it to happen to anyone else.

As the fight intensified, the atmosphere crackled with tension. The once perfect environment now resembled a battlefield. The sound of metal clashing against metal filled the air as James and his crew leader fought for life and death. The chaos of their clash created a sensory overload. Sparks exploded from damaged electrical wires, illuminating the scene with brief flashes of light.

As Henry stood guard, his senses sharpened, ready to respond to any potential threat. The weight of re-sponsibility pressed upon him, knowing that he held the power to control who entered and exited the room. It was a duty he took seriously, his loyalty unwavering as he protected James and maintained the integrity of their mission.

In the midst of this heightened tension, a shot rang
out, sending shockwaves through the room. James
instinctively flinched, his heart racing as he believed
the shot was intended for him. Confusion clouded his
mind as he dealt with the possibility of betrayal from
his trusted friend. However, as the echo of the gunshot
subsided, James realized that the bullet had missed him,
a chilling reminder of the instability of their situation.
His eyes darted towards Henry, searching for an explanation, desperately seeking to understand the intentions
behind the shot.

Henry's face remained calm, his eyes locked on James
with a mix of determination and urgency. It was an intended move, a warning shot fired not at James, but rather in the direction from which potential threats might
occur. The intention was not to harm his friend but
to ensure their safety by maintaining control over who
entered the room. Understanding dawned upon James
as he comprehended Henry's strategy. Though the initial
shock and confusion lingered, he recognized the depth
of Henry's commitment to their shared mission. It was a
demonstration of Henry's solid dedication to protecting
their operation and ensuring their survival. Realization
settled in, James's gaze locked with Henry's, and a silent
acknowledgment passed between them. At this moment,
Henry's actions spoke volumes, solidifying the bond of
trust that had been forged through countless trials.

The harsh smell of burning insulation mixed with
the scent of gunpowder, creating a volatile combination
that lingered in the air. The room was submerged in

                                    JOY M PIERRE

a cloud of smoke, flowing from collapsing structures, weakening their vision. James had to carefully choose his stability, avoiding unstable sections of the floor and the dangerous debris that threatened to trip him up. However, despite the obstacles, he moved with an almost dancer like grace, and his body adjusted to the unstable environment.

With every strike and block, James used his surroundings to his advantage. He utilized the crumbling structures as cover, ducking behind fallen pillars or crumbling walls to shield himself from being attacked. The sparks from damaged wires became his allies, providing momentary flashes of light that allowed him to anticipate his opponent's movement.

The clashing of their weapons echoed through the space, each gun fire delivered with accuracy. James' movements were swift and deliberate, his attacks making a loud impact. Adrenaline surged through James' veins, intensifying his senses and perfecting his focus. He was in his element, a master of invention within the chaos. Each obstacle he encountered became an opportunity, a stepping stone towards victory.

In the midst of the escalating battle, exhaustion began to take its toll on James. The smoke thickened, swirling around him, obstructing his vision and making each breath a struggle. The air grew heavy with the bitter scent of destruction, and every movement became a difficult task. However, fueled by his firm determination, James pressed forward. He and the crew leader circled

each other, their movements were calculated and deliberate. Fatigue weighed heavily on their shoulders, but
their determination was unbending. With each passing
moment, their lungs fought desperately for air, the toxic
environment threatening to overpower them. Yet, James
refused to surrender to the suffocating surroundings. In
a burst of adrenaline, James made a daring dash towards
the door, his muscles screaming in protest. The journey
felt like an eternity as his legs grew heavier with every
step. He could feel his body staggering on the edge of
collapse, but his mind remained focused.

Reaching the locked door, James's trembling hands
fumbled with the lock, his vision blurred by sweat and
exhaustion. His heart pounded in his chest, each beat
a reminder of the precious seconds slipping away. In a
desperate bid for freedom, he raised his gun and fired at
the lock, the echoing gunshot muffled through the chaos.
With a resounding crack, the lock shattered, and James
gathered the last bits and pieces of his strength to kick
the door open. As the door swung wide, fresh air rushed
in, filling his lungs and Henry was right behind him
coughing. Gasping for breath, James stumbled forward,
embracing the coolness of the outside world against his
sweaty skin.

For a brief moment, James allowed himself to smell
the taste of freedom and the victory of survival. And as
James savored the fleeting taste of freedom, a sudden
commotion erupted behind him. Startled, he turned his
head just in time to see the crew leader emerge from
the chaos, pushing past both James and Henry with

                                        JOY M PIERRE

desperate determination engraved on his face. Without a second thought, the crew leader sprinted towards his waiting car, the engine roaring to life.

At that moment, James felt a surge of conflicting emotions. The battle had taken its toll, physically and mentally, but the crew leader's escape threatened to undo all their efforts. It was a critical moment, and James knew that decisive action was required to prevent their enemy from slipping away.

Shaking off his fatigue, James's instincts kicked into high gear. He mustered every ounce of strength remaining within him and sprinted after the crew leader, his mind laser focused on capturing him from escaping. The adrenaline flowing through his veins fueled his determination, drowning out the fatigue that threatened to overwhelm him. With each stride, James closed the gap between himself and the fleeing crew leader. The world around him blurred, and his senses enhanced in on the pursuit as if time itself had slowed down. The uproar of the battle faded away, replaced by the rhythmic pounding of his own heart. As James closed in on the crew leader, his thoughts raced, calculating his next move. With a burst of energy, he lunged forward, his outstretched arm reaching for the crew leader's shoulder. In a frantic attempt to halt the escape, James' fingers grazed the fabric of the crew leader's jacket, but it slipped through his grip with the momentum carrying him forward. He turned his focus to the crew leader's car, which had been roaring to life, exhaust fumes flowing into the air. With a surge of adrenaline, James sprinted towards the vehicle, his mind still racing to find a way to prevent the crew leader's escape.

In a split second decision, James's hand instinctively dove into his pocket, fingers closing around the small, specially crafted device he had prepared for emergencies. With a surge of adrenaline and his mind focused on stopping the crew leader's escape, he threw the device with practiced precision toward the rear bumper of the fleeing car. Time seemed to slow as the device soared through the air, spinning with controlled determination. It connected with the car's bumper, latching onto its surface with a satisfying click. In an instant, the tires screeched as the car stalled, slowing down; a piece of evidence to the success of James' created device.

Hope swelled within James' chest as he closed the distance between himself and the powerless vehicle. The victory was within reach, and the crew leader was on the urge of being caught. As the crew leader attempted to regain control of the immobilized car, a sharp bump in the road sent a jolt through the vehicle's frame. At that moment, the device, designed to restrain the vehicle was dislodged from the bumper, its grip weakened by the unexpected impact. The device flew off the car's surface, tumbling through the air before smashing onto the pavement. James watched in disbelief as his once great device plan unraveled before his eyes. The crew leader snatched back the opportunity to escape, no longer hindered by the ineffective device.

A mix of frustration and disappointment surged

                                        JOY M PIERRE

through James as he realized the crew leader had slipped through their hands and gotten away. The fleeting taste of victory transformed into a bitter aftertaste of missed opportunity. However, in the face of this setback, James' determination remained.

With a firm shake of his head, James refocused his attention. He knew they couldn't afford to dwell on what was lost. The crew leader may have escaped capture at that time, but the battle was far from over. Regrouping with Henry, their eyes locked in silent understanding. Undeterred, they recommitted themselves to the task at hand, fueled by a renewed sense of purpose. They would redouble their efforts, recalibrate their strategy, and relentlessly continue to go after the crew leader. As they stood within the fallen device, the scene well-lit by the glowing streetlights, James's mind raced with possibilities. He knew that the crew leader's escape would only serve to strengthen their determination and fuel their willpower to get him.

Yet, just as they walked away, their footsteps heavy with purpose, a deafening explosion ripped through the air. The ground trembled beneath them, and in an instant, the world spun into chaos. James and Henry were thrown violently to the ground, their bodies battered by the force of the blast. When James regained consciousness, he found himself lying in a sterile hospital room, surrounded by the steady hum of medical equipment. The pain burned through his body, a stark reminder of the injuries he had sustained. Confusion and disorientation clouded his mind, but his determination remained steady. As he pieced together the fragments of his memory, the truth crashed down upon him like a tidal wave. The explosion had been a set trap, a cruel plot orchestrated by their own crew leader. In that moment, the weight of guilt and sorrow settled heavily upon James once again.

The realization hit him with a staggering force about Henry, his friend and partner, had made the ultimate sacrifice to save James' life. Henry saw a timer ticking down from three seconds, and pushed James away from what appeared to be a bomb. Henry paid the ultimate price with his life.

The weight of guilt and sorrow bore down on James' chest, threatening to suffocate him, knowing Henry had made an ultimate sacrifice for him to live. James spent several weeks in the hospital recovering from his injuries. He underwent several surgeries to repair broken bones and damaged tissue, and he had to undergo painful physical therapy to regain strength in his body too. The loss of his friend Henry kept weighing heavily on him. He knew if it wasn't for Henry pushing him away, it could have been his life instead of his long-time friend. James swore to make sure that Henry's sacrifice was not in vain and that he would make their crew leader pay for the pain he caused.

# Chapter 5

Janet was horrified and didn't know what to do. Her heart pounded in her chest as she watched the news unfold before her eyes. Janet's hands also trembled as she clenched them into fists, her mind racing with regret and determination. She couldn't bear the weight of her past actions any longer. With a firm determination burning in her eyes, Janet made a vow to herself. She would correct her mistakes, not just for the sake of her own conscience, but for James and the countless others who had suffered at the hands of the criminal organization. It was time for her to step out of the shadows and take an active role in dismantling the empire that had caused so much pain.

Janet's mind raced as she struggled to comprehend the dual identity of the crew leader, who had been masquerading as her trusted psychiatrist. The weight of betrayal and deceit stirred her up, intensifying her determination to interrogate him.

With her skilled hacker friend Alex by her side, Janet began digging deeper into the crew leader's background, searching for any past information that could shed light on his true nature. They dug into archived records, online databases, and even reached out to confidential sources, piecing together a disturbing puzzle of his dark past. As they uncovered more about the crew leader's history, a pattern emerged. His psychiatric profession had served as a perfect cover to exploit vulnerable individuals, gaining their trust while covertly involving them in criminal activities. Janet realized that she wasn't the only victim of his manipulative tactics. Others had unknowingly become tangled in his web of tricks and suffered the consequences like Henry. Janet and Alex, driven by their determination to protect others from the crew leader's schemes, set their plan in motion. They knew that exposing the crew leader's criminal activities would require careful execution and gathering substantial evidence that would leave no room for doubt.

Their first step was to reach out to the victims who had unknowingly fallen into the crew leader's web. They connected with them discreetly, offering support and sharing their own experiences. Janet wanted to ensure that each victim felt safe and supported, knowing that they were not alone in their struggle. She wanted to form a coalition of survivors who were willing to share their stories and cooperate in the pursuit of justice. Janet knew that their collective voices would carry more weight and make it harder for the crew leader to escape the consequences of his actions, but no one was willing to go against him. In the shadows, Janet and Alex gathered evidence, documenting every illicit transaction, every manipulation, and every act of coercion perpetrated by the crew leader. They dug deep into the digital realm, uncovering hidden financial transactions, falsified records, and connections to other criminal entities.

In the dimly lit room, Janet and Alex sat hunched over their computers, their eyes fixed on the screens before them. The sound of rapid keystrokes echoed through the space as they precisely gathered evidence against the crew leader. Every illegal transaction, every manipulation, and every act of coercion were accurately documented. Alex skillfully bypassed the secure firewall and breached secure servers, leaving no stone unturned in their hunt for incriminating evidence. The atmosphere was tense, and they were determined to dig as deep as it took to uncover the crew leader's operations.

As the hours turned into days, Janet's eyes burned with exhaustion, but she refused to give in. The weight of responsibility pressed upon her shoulders, driving her forward. She knew that uncovering the truth was not just about seeking justice for the victims but also about protecting countless others who might become entangled in the crew leader's web of dishonesty. Their efforts began to bear fruit as hidden financial transactions were exposed, revealing the crew leader's vast wealth accumulated through illegal means. Janet and Alex traced the flow of money, connecting the dots between falsified records, and offshore accounts. Each piece of evidence they uncovered served as a critical piece of the puzzle. But it didn't end there. Through their digital investigation, they also discovered connections to other criminal entities, intertwining webs of corruption that extended far beyond what they had initially anticipated. The scope of the crew leader's operations was larger than they had imagined, reaching into the darkest corners of the criminal underworld.

The tension in the room grew intense as Janet and Alex realized the risks they were taking. They were getting closer to exposing a dangerous individual with power and influence, someone who would stop at nothing to protect their empire. But the knowledge of the victims' suffering and the desire for justice pushed them forward, overriding their fears.

One night, as Janet and Alex dug deeper into the crew leader's network, their screens flickered with a sudden surge of data. They had stumbled upon a heavily encrypted file, seemingly holding the key to unraveling the crew leader's entire operation. They initiated the decryption process, their fingers dancing across the keyboard. Time seemed to slow as the progress bar inched forward. Each passing second heightened the anticipation, the air thick with expectancy. Finally, as the decryption was completed, the file revealed its secrets. The screen was filled with incriminating evidence, detailed records of the crew leader's activities, and a list of accomplices involved in his criminal empire. Janet and Alex exchanged a glance, their eyes filled with a mix of accomplishment and nervousness.

Janet's heart sank as her computer abruptly shut down, plunging the room into a creepy silence. Panic surged through her veins as she realized they had been discovered. The hackers from the crew leader's organization had intervened, swiftly cutting off their access to the incriminating evidence they had uncovered.

Gathering her thoughts, Janet quickly assessed the situation. She knew they had to act quickly before the crew leader's organization could trace their location or erase the evidence they had collected. With a calm yet determined expression, she turned to Alex, their eyes meeting with unspoken understanding. Without wasting a moment, they sprang into action, activating their contingency plan. Alex swiftly disconnected their compromised computer from the network, isolating it from any further intrusion attempts. Meanwhile, Janet took instructions from him on how to activate a secondary encrypted communication channel to reach out to their trusted allies, sharing the news of the breach.

As they worked together under intense pressure, Janet and Alex devised a countermeasure to deactivate the crew leader's hackers. They analyzed their opponent's methods, recognizing patterns and vulnerabilities that could be abused. Their previous experiences in uncovering the crew leader's secrets proved invaluable as they strategized their next move. Utilizing their skills and resources, Alex launched a tit-for-tat cyberattack, aiming to cripple the crew leader's organization's defenses.

They targeted their infrastructure, exploiting weaknesses and launching a barrage of complicated digital tricks. It was a battle of intellect and technical skills. The tension mounted as the seconds ticked by. Janet and Alex fought tooth and nail, their determination firm. They were driven by the urgency of their mission and the lives of others. Failure was not an option.

Finally, with the evidence safely secured, Janet disconnected the backup device and prepared for their escape. They knew they couldn't stay in one location for long. The crew leader hackers were persistent, and every passing moment increased the risk of discovery. Janet and Alex hastily gathered their belongings and exited their current hideout, leaving behind no trace of their presence. Their escape route involved a series of carefully coordinated steps and multiple safe houses strategically located across the city. Each safe house offered a brief break, allowing them to rest, regroup, and plan their next move. As they navigated through the complicated city, Janet's senses remained heightened. She felt the weight of responsibility on her shoulders, knowing that their safety and the success of their mission relied on her. Janet and Alex hurried through the dimly lit streets, their footsteps echoing off the buildings. The adrenaline flowing through their veins kept them from being fatigued while running through the city, their eyes scanning their surroundings for any signs of danger.

As they reached the next safe house, a run down building tucked away in an abandoned alley, Janet's instincts kicked in. Something felt off. The door was slightly open, a thin line of light seeping through the crack. She motioned for Alex to stop, her hand hovering above her pistol, strapped to her thigh. With a silent nod, they approached cautiously. Janet pushed the door open, her heart pounding in her chest. As they stepped inside, their worst fears were confirmed. The safe house had been compromised. Furniture was overturned, papers scattered across the floor, and the air carried a lingering scent of burnt electronics. Janet's mind raced, desperately trying to piece together what went wrong. They had been careful in covering their tracks, leaving no trace behind. They had encrypted their communications, shuffled their routes, and taken all necessary precautions. Making it near impossible for the crew leader hackers to find them.

Suddenly, the sound of shattering glass exploded from the adjacent room. Janet and Alex exchanged a tense squint and instinctively ducked behind a nearby counter. Janet reached for her weapon, ready to defend them against whatever threat awaited them. From the corner of her eye, Janet spotted a group of armed figures dressed in black tactical gear, moving swiftly through the broken doorway. It was the crew leader hackers, their cold gazes fixated on their targets. Without a moment's hesitation, Janet sprang into action. She unleashed a ton of bullets toward the evolving enemies, using the scattered furniture as cover. The room blew up into chaos, the booming sound of gunfire rumbling off the walls. She moved with precision, her shots finding their marks as she expertly moved throughout the room. But the crew leader hackers were relentless. They were well-trained and equipped, matching Janet's every move. The battle continued, each side exchanging gunfire, ducking, and weaving through the chaos.

Janet's heart pounded in her chest as she fought on, her determination unwavering. She couldn't give up. She couldn't let the crew leader hackers get their hands on the evidence they had risked so much to obtain. As the clash continued, Janet noticed a spark of light in her peripheral vision. She spotted a ventilation shaft high above, a potential escape route. With a swift gesture, she signaled Alex, who nodded in understanding. They disengaged from the firefight, taking advantage of a momentary pause in the chaos. With calculated precision, they made their way toward the ventilation shaft, evading the enemy's line of sight. The crew leader hackers realized their plan too late, unleashing a hail of bullets toward them as they disappeared into the narrow passage. Janet's heart raced as they crawled through the cramped shaft, their bodies pressed against the cold metal. The sound of gunfire and shouting echoed from the room they had just left behind. The crew leader hackers would soon discover their escape, and the chase would continue.

Reaching the end of the ventilation shaft, they emerged onto the roof of the building. They quickly scanned the area, searching for a way down. Spotting a fire escape ladder nearby, they sprinted toward it, adrenaline fueling their movements. They hurried down the ladder with determination, their footsteps echoing off the alley walls. Once they reached the ground, they melted into the crowded streets, blending in with the city's fast life. Janet's senses remained heightened, her eyes darting from person to person, aware that the crew leader hackers could be lurking anywhere. With their evidence safely secured, Janet knew they had to regroup, reassess their situation, and strengthen their defenses.

The crew leader hackers had proven themselves to be intimidating enemies, and Janet was determined to outsmart them. As they disappeared into the crowded streets, Janet couldn't help but feel a mixture of relief and urgency. They had narrowly escaped, but the mistake that had led the crew leader hackers to them still haunted her. She vowed to uncover the leak within their ranks and ensure their next move would be one step ahead. The cat-and-mouse game had just intensified as Janet and Alex blend was fading and their pace quickened, their bodies moving with purpose. They knew they couldn't afford to linger in one place for long, as the crew leader hackers were persistent in their hunt. Their next safe house was situated across town, hidden within the maze-like alleyways of the old district.

They navigated through the streets, their senses on high alert. Janet's instincts enhanced over the countless missions, guided by their every step, ensuring they remained undetected. But the crew leader hackers were sneaky. Janet sensed their presence, the feeling of being watched intensifying. She discreetly signaled Alex, prompting him to adjust their route. They turned off into a narrow alley, their pace quickening as they plunged deeper into the street maze. Suddenly, the quietness shattered as a group of armed hackers emerged from the shadows, blocking their path. Janet's heart skipped a beat. They had walked right into an ambush.

Without hesitation, Janet and Alex sprang into action. Bullets whizzed through the air as they sought cover behind rusted metal barrels and discarded crates. Janet returned fire, her shots precise and calculated. The alley became a battlefield, echoing with the sound of gunfire. Janet's mind raced as she assessed the situation. They were outnumbered, and their enemies seemed to have the upper hand in terms of firepower.

She knew they had to think quickly and utilize their surroundings to turn the tide. With a nod of understanding, Janet and Alex separated, their movements coordinated like a well-choreographed dance. She launched herself from behind cover, executing a flawless somersault that surprised the attackers. Her hands moved with practiced precision, deploying a series of hidden gadgets she carried, momentarily disorienting their foes. Smoke grenades enveloped the alley, filling it with a thick haze that obscured their vision. Taking advantage of the chaos, Alex took off running in the opposite direction, weapons blazing toward him, missing his every step. The clash of metal and the thump of bodies hitting the ground echoed, earthquake style.

The sound of sirens wailed in the distance, growing louder with each passing moment. Janet knew their window of opportunity was closing rapidly. With renewed urgency, she grabbed her weapon and quickly moved

                           JOY M PIERRE

away in the same direction as Alex, blending back into the crowd that paraded down the sidewalk. She kept her head down, her movements casual, but inside, she was thinking about their next move. The police presence meant that the crew leader hackers had managed to tip them off, further confirming the existence of a leak. She glanced back briefly, ensuring Alex was by her side, and they continued to move through the crowd, putting as much distance as possible between themselves and the alley. Janet's mind raced, contemplating their options. They needed to find a safe place to regroup and reassess their situation. The compromised safe house was out of the question now. Spotting a discreet entrance to an underground subway station up ahead, Janet made a split-second decision. She led Alex toward it, their pace quickening as they descended into the tunnels below.

The ear-piercing rumble of trains filled their ears as they emerged onto a crowded platform. The constant flow of people offered them a level of discretion they desperately needed. Janet's gaze scanned the surroundings, searching for any signs of potential danger. A spark of movement caught her eye. Through the swarm of commuters, she spotted a familiar face. It was the mysterious figure known only as "The Fixer." The Fixer was a legendary underground contact, renowned for their ability to assist those in need with escape routes, forged documents, and safe houses. Janet's heart skipped a beat. This encounter couldn't be a coincidence. Without hesitation, she nudged Alex, slightly directing his attention toward The Fixer. Wordlessly, they approached the figure, weaving their way through the crowd.

The Fixer's eyes met Janet's, a knowing glint in their gaze. They nodded, acknowledging their presence, and seamlessly fell into sync beside them, their movements blending effortlessly with the busy commuters. The Fixer led them through a maze of tunnels, their knowledge of the underground network proving invaluable. All three of them emerged into a hidden safe house, tucked away beneath the city streets. Janet couldn't help but feel a sense of relief wash over her as they entered the secure location. Inside, the air was thick with anticipation. The Fixer wasted no time, gathering their resources and connecting them to a network of like-minded individuals who would provide support in the face of the crew leader hackers' relentless pursuit.

As Janet shared their recent encounters and the betrayal that had led the hackers to them, she could see the gears turning in The Fixer's mind. They understood the gravity of the situation, and the urgent need to uncover the leak within their ranks. With strong determination, The Fixer devised a plan; a plan that would put them one step ahead of their enemies. Janet and Alex listened intently, strengthening their persistence with each word. The cat-and-mouse game had reached a new level, but Janet was ready. The crew leader hackers had mistaken her once, but she would not make the same mistake again. The tide was about to turn, and the true strength of their association would be revealed. As the safe house buzzed with activity, Janet's mind focused on the upcoming challenges to protect her team at all costs.

Janet's heart skipped a beat as her phone vibrated,

indicating an incoming call from James, even though they haven't spoken to each other in a while. She quickly excused herself from the full of commotion safe house and stepped into a secluded corner, answering the call with a sense of urgency.

"James, what's going on?" Janet asked, her voice laced with concern.

"Janet, the situation has taken a turn for the worse," James replied, his tone filled with worry. "The police have discovered that I was planning a heist. And they want me to go to the police station for questioning. You wouldn't have anything to do with this, would you?"

Janet's heart sank at James's words. The situation had taken an unexpected and dangerous twist. She had hoped to protect James from the dangers that surrounded her, but it seemed that he had become entangled in the web of consequences.

"No, James," Janet replied firmly, her voice laced with sincerity. "I had nothing to do with this. I'm sorry you're caught up in it, but I promise you, I will do everything I can to help you."

The urgency of the situation heightened as she realized that the police were closing in on James. Time was of the essence, and they needed to act swiftly to keep him out of their control.

"Listen carefully, James," Janet continued, her mind

racing with possibilities. "I need you to trust me on this one. I know a place where we can lay low, at least for a while. Meet me at the main floor lobby in one hour. And we'll figure out a plan to get you out of this mess."

As the call ended, Janet's mind shifted gears. She quickly returned and gathered Alex and The Fixer, sharing the urgent situation with them. The stakes had risen, and they needed to prioritize James' safety while still pursuing their mission against the crew leader hackers.

Together, they formulated a new plan; a plan that involved diverting tactics and skillful hacking exercises. They also created a distraction, allowing James to slip away from the hospital unnoticed and meet Janet at the designated location. The distraction they planned involved hacking into the hospital's security system and creating a false alarm in another wing. This would draw the attention of the staff and provide a window of opportunity for James to slip away unnoticed.

Alex took charge of the diversion, utilizing their expertise to manipulate the hospital's surveillance cameras, alarms, and communication systems. They worked swiftly and silently, leaving no trace of their digital intrusion. Meanwhile, Janet made her way to the hospital, her heart pounding with a mix of anxiety and determination. She carefully navigated the corridors, avoiding any suspicious glances from hospital personnel. As chaos erupted in the designated wing due to the diversion, Janet spotted James in his hospital room, panicking and afraid to leave. She rushed to his side, a mixture of relief and worry

                    JOY M PIERRE

flooding her senses.

"James, we don't have much time," Janet whispered sarcastically. "We need to get you out of here before they realize what's happening. Can you walk, or do you need a wheelchair?"

James nodded, his face pale but filled with determination. He swung his legs over the edge of the bed and stood up, although with a slight wince of pain. Together, they moved quickly and quietly, avoiding any potential encounters with hospital staff or security personnel. Using her knowledge of the hospital's layout and the information provided by Alex, Janet led James through a series of back corridors and service entrances, avoiding detection at every turn. Finally, they reached a secluded exit, concealed from the prying eyes of the hospital's security cameras. Alex had ensured that the area was temporarily blind to surveillance, providing them with a crucial advantage. With a deep breath, Janet pushed open the door, and they stepped out into the cool night air.

They were free; for now. But the danger was far from over. Janet's mind raced with thoughts of their next move. They needed to regroup with The Fixer and the rest of their team, ensuring that they were all safely reunited and ready to face the challenges ahead. As Janet and James hurried through the dimly lit streets, their senses remained heightened. They knew they had to remain vigilant, for the crew leader hackers and the police were relentless in their pursuit. Finally, they arrived at the designated meeting point; a safe house tucked away in a quiet neighborhood. The lights inside were dim, and the air crackled with a sense of urgency. Janet pushed open the door, and they stepped inside, greeted by the familiar faces of their teammates. The Fixer, Alex, and the rest of the team were gathered, their expressions a mix of concern and relief.

"We made it," Janet said, her voice filled with determination. "But our mission is not over. We need to stay focused, uncover the leak within our ranks, and bring down the crew leader hackers. Together, we are stronger, and we will not rest until this is all over."

The room fell silent as her words hung in the air, fueling the fire within each member of the team. The true strength of their association had been tested, but they were ready to face whatever challenges lay ahead. The tide was turning, and the crew leader hackers would soon realize the mistake they had made by underestimating Janet and her team.

# Chapter 6

Janet woke up one night, threw the blanket off, and slipped on her shoes that she placed under her bed. Her mind raced with determination as she quietly slipped out of the safe house, careful not to disturb her sleeping teammates. But as soon as the door closed, Alex opened his eyes. She knew the risks of going solo, but the weight of responsibility urged her forward. There was a fire burning within her, a burning need to take action and ensure the success of their mission. Under the cover of darkness, Janet moved swiftly through the deserted streets, her senses heightened. She had formulated a new plan, one that required precision and sneakiness. The crew leader hackers had proven themselves to be formidable adversaries, and Janet was determined to outdo them.

Her first destination was a high-security facility, believed to house the encrypted data backups of the crew leader hackers. If she could obtain those backups, it would provide important evidence to expose their true identities and dismantle their operation. Alex didn't teach her everything but he did teach her enough to be dangerous. So her knowledge of intrusion and hacking techniques served her well as she navigated the facility's complex security systems. She expertly bypassed surveillance cameras, disabled motion sensors, and avoided patrolling guards. Every step was planned, every movement deliberate. As she made her way to the control room, Janet's heart pounded in her chest. The pressure mounted with each passing moment, knowing that any mistake could jeopardize the entire operation and potentially have her killed. But she pushed forward, fueled by a fierce determination to protect her team and bring the crew leader hackers down.

Inside the control room, Janet accessed the main computer terminal. She swiftly hacked into the facility's network, searching for encrypted data backups. The seconds felt like an eternity as she bypassed complex encryption algorithms and security protocols. Finally, the encrypted backups appeared on the screen before her, ready to be extracted. With practiced efficiency, Janet transferred the data onto a secure device she had brought with her. But as she disconnected the device, an alarm suddenly blared throughout the facility. Janet's heart skipped a beat. Her actions had been detected, and time was running out.

She raced out of the control room, adrenaline surging through her veins. The facility went on high alert, with guards mobilizing to intercept her. Janet's training kicked in as she employed evasive maneuvers, darting through corridors and utilizing her surroundings to her advantage. She fought her way through waves of security personnel, disabling them with precise strikes. Every move was fueled by her unwavering determination to protect the evidence and secure her escape. As Janet burst out of the facility's main entrance, a side-view image of her face was caught on the camera. She sprinted into the night, clutching the device containing the encrypted data. She knew that her actions would have consequences, and she couldn't afford to rest until the evidence was safely delivered. With every step taken, Janet grew stronger. She had taken a risk by going solo, but she was determined to prove her worth and guarantee the success of the mission. As Janet disappeared into the shadows to reunite with her team, she was stopped. A dark-colored SUV screeched to a halt, blocking Janet's path as she appeared from the shadows. Automatically, she tightened her grip on the device containing the encrypted data, ready to defend herself if necessary. The tinted window of the SUV rolled down slowly, revealing a stern-faced individual behind the wheel.

"Janet, we need to talk," a familiar voice resonated from within the vehicle.

Janet's heart skipped a beat. She recognized that voice all too well. It was James. Conflicting emotions surged through her; relief at seeing a familiar face, but also suspicious given the delicate situation she was in.

"James? What are you doing here?" Janet asked, her voice filled with a mixture of surprise and caution.

"Get in the car, Janet. We don't have much time," James replied urgently, his eyes darting around, scanning the surroundings for any signs of trouble.

Janet hesitated for a moment, weighing her options. Trusting James was a risk, but perhaps he held valuable information or a crucial role in the unfolding events. With a final glance over her shoulder, Janet cautiously approached the SUV and climbed into the passenger seat, keeping the device with the evidence a secret. When James turned his head, Janet slowly push the device into the bottom corner of her pocket so it wasn't noticeable.

As the car sped away, James quickly explained the situation. It turned out that he had been keeping tabs on the crew leader hackers, gathering information covertly while pretending to be under their control. His intention had been to find a way to dismantle their operation from within.

"I've discovered something big, Janet," James said, his voice filled with determination. "There's a mole within our ranks, someone feeding information to the crew leader hackers. That's how they keep finding us." Janet's eyes widened in shock and disbelief.

"A mole," Janet yelled.

It was devastating, but it also provided an explanation for the crew leader hackers' mysterious ability to anticipate their moves.

"We need to find out who the mole is and expose them," Janet declared, with her firm voice. "We cannot continue like this, constantly on the run, constantly one step behind."

James nodded in agreement, his gaze fixed on the road ahead. They knew that their next move had to be precise and well-executed. Lives were at stake, and the safety of their entire operation relied on their ability to uncover the traitor in their midst. Together, Janet and James devised a plan, utilizing their combined skills, knowledge, and resources. Their primary objective was to identify the mole and gather concrete evidence to expose them to the rest of the team. It was a risky endeavor, but they were determined to protect their buddies and bring an end to the crew leader hackers. As the SUV raced through the city streets, Janet's mind focused on the task ahead. The tide had shifted once again, and the challenges they faced had become even more double-crossing. But with James by her side, Janet felt a sense of renewal, even though she wasn't letting him in on her highjacked information on the device. But if Janet and James were amongst a traitor, the traitor probably knew when the alarm sounded at the facility that it could have been either one of them or both because they disappeared and wasn't where he last seen them.

Making it back to the safe house, Janet and James walked in normally, perpetrating as if they had been out for a late night date, by laughing and talking on the way in. Inside the safe house, the atmosphere was tense. The rest of the team had awaken, and were unaware of Janet and James' true intentions, greeted them with cautious glances and suspicious eyes. Janet knew that they had to play their parts convincingly if they were to flush out the mole. As they mingled with the team, Janet discreetly observed their behaviors, searching for any signs of un-ease or abnormality. She had to trust her instincts, rely-ing on her experience as a hacker and her ability to read people. She couldn't afford to be wrong this time. The safe house buzzed with activity, conversations flowing, and plans being discussed. Janet discreetly slipped away, making her way to the control room where the security footage and communications were monitored. She need-ed to access the system without arousing suspicion.

James, on the other hand, engaged in casual conver-sations with the team members, carefully probing for any hints or slip-ups that might reveal the identity of the mole. His charm and affable nature masked his true purpose, gaining the trust of his buddies as he gath-ered information. Janet bypassed security measures, her fingers flying across the keyboard as she dug deeper into the system. She scanned through surveillance footage, communication logs, and any other digital traces that might lead her to the traitor. Time was of the essence, and she needed to find the evidence before the mole had a chance to cover their tracks. As the minutes ticked by, Janet's heart pounded in her chest. Every passing second

increased the risk of discovery, but she was determined
to uncover the truth. Finally, her efforts paid off. She
discovered a series of encrypted messages hidden within the system, indicating secret communication with an
external source. With her heart racing, Janet decrypted
the messages and her eyes widened in shock. The name
of the mole stared back at her from the screen, sending
a chill down her spine. It was someone she least expected, someone she had considered a trusted ally. While
still there, she dug into the bottom of her pocket, pulled
out the device, and shoved it into the computer with
force. As the device was loading, a jingle at the door
knob started her. She yanked the device out and walked
over to the file cabinets, shoving it back into her pocket
pretending to look for an old file. She was greeted by a
team member entering the room. It was Tim, another
skilled hacker whom she had been friends with since
her college days. Janet's heart raced, wondering why Tim
followed her. She forced a smile, trying to hide the confusion inside her.

"Hey, Tim," she greeted, her voice slightly trembling.
"Just going through some old files here. Can I help you
with something?"

Tim looked at her curiously, a hint of suspicion in
his eyes. "No, just came in to grab a few things. Is everything alright? You seem a bit tense."

Janet brushed off his concern, hoping to maintain
her composure. "Oh, it's nothing. Just a long night, you
know? Trying to piece together some information. It can

get a bit overwhelming sometimes."

Tim nodded, seemingly satisfied with her explanation. "Yeah, I understand. Well, don't stress too much. We'll get through this together."

As Tim left the room, Janet took a deep breath, trying to steady her racing thoughts. She needed to be cautious, to act as if she had found nothing out of the ordinary. There was no room for missteps or false accusations. Returning to her task, Janet resumed her investigation, carefully documenting the evidence she had uncovered. The encrypted messages she had decrypted pointed directly to Tim's involvement. It was a devastating exposure, as Tim had been a trusted member of their team. Janet's heart skipped a beat as Tim barged back into the room, his face twisted with anger and betrayal. He had caught her red-handed, with the evidence of his betrayal laid bare before him. The atmosphere in the room turned tense, the air thick with unspoken tension.

Tim's eyes darted between Janet and the incriminating files displayed on the computer screen. His face twisted into a mix of disbelief and fury. He clenched his fists, his voice trembling with suppressed rage.

"I knew you were up to something, Janet?" Tim snarled, his voice laced with hatred. "You've been digging into my personal files? Spying on me?

Janet's mind raced, trying to come up with a reasonable explanation. She knew that any wrong move could

                              JOY M PIERRE

lead to terrible consequences, not just for her but for the entire team. She took a deep breath, maintaining a composed cover-up despite the adrenaline coursing through her veins.

"Tim, calm down," Janet replied, her voice steady. "I stumbled upon these files by accident. I didn't know they were yours. I was just trying to piece together some information for our mission."

Tim sighed, his eyes narrowing in suspicion. "Accident? Don't play dumb, Janet. I trusted you, and this is how you repay me by going behind my back?"

Janet met Tim's stare with a mixture of determination and regret. "Tim, I don't know what you're involved in, but these files contain encrypted messages that point to your communication with the crew leader hackers. I had to investigate to protect the team."

Tim's face paled, the color draining from his features. He realized that somehow he was linked to betrayal and Janet was telling the rest of the team. The room fell into a heavy silence, the tension between them thickening. Suddenly, the sound of approaching footsteps echoed outside the room, indicating the arrival of the rest of the team. Janet knew that she had to act quickly to prevent further chaos and ensure their safety. So she quickly hit the print button sending all the documents to a printer in a different location, and closed all the windows as if nothing was happening. "Tim, we need to talk, but not here," Janet said, her voice lowered to a whisper. "Let's step outside and handle this discreetly. We don't want to raise unnecessary suspicion."

Tim hesitated for a moment, his stare flickering with uncertainty. Unwillingly, he nodded, realizing that the situation had escalated beyond repair. They exited the room together, keeping their conversation quiet. As they moved to a more secluded area, Janet maintained her composure, her mind working on how to handle the delicate situation.

"Janet," Tim replied, his voice tinged with determination. "I don't know how this happened, but we need to find out who is framing me and threatening our mission. I'm innocent."

At the same time in suspicion, James saw the both of them leaving the room and followed. As James silently trailed behind Janet and Tim, he maintained a careful distance, making sure not to stir any suspicion. His footsteps were light, and he skillfully navigated the hallways, keeping his senses sharp. He knew the importance of remaining unnoticed, as any misstep could jeopardize whatever they planned and the reason he was following them. They both led James through a maze of hallways, their pace quickening as they reached a secluded area, it was where multiple printers were kept.

James observed from a hidden vantage point as Janet and Tim engaged in a hushed conversation, their expressions serious and focused. He strained his ears, trying to catch bits of their conversation to piece together their intentions. Just as he was about to move closer to gain a better understanding, he noticed a flicker of movement from the corner of his eye. A security guard was making his rounds to protect the safe house, coming dangerously close to their location. James instinctively pressed himself against the wall, blending into the shadows, his heart pounding in his chest. The security guard's footsteps echoed through the hall, growing louder with each passing second. James held his breath, praying that he wouldn't be discovered. The guard paused for a moment, as if sensing someone nearby, but then continued on his patrol without giving it a further thought.

As the guard disappeared around the corner, James let out a sigh of relief. He knew he couldn't afford any more close calls. With renewed determination, he cautiously approached Janet and Tim, careful not to startle them.

"Janet, Tim," James whispered, his voice barely audible. "Hey, I saw the both of leaving, and wanted to check on you. Do you need help?"

Startled and shocked, Janet and Tim turned to face James, their eyes widening in surprise. They exchanged glances, silently acknowledging that James was there.

"James, we didn't expect to see you here," Janet said, her voice filled with gratitude. "We could definitely use your help. We're on the verge of uncovering a mole that we were looking for."

James nodded in agreement, his eyes focused and determined. "Absolutely. We need to gather as much evidence as possible to ensure the safety of our team. I've been gathering information on the crew leader hackers, and I believe it's connected to a mole too."

Janet grabbed the documents from the printer, rolling them into a flute, while James and Tim watched.

Next, Janet and Tim exchanged a quick glance, as his trust in James grew stronger with each passing moment. They decided to find another secure location within the safe house, away from prying eyes and potential eavesdroppers to go over the evidence. Sitting around a table, they laid out the printouts they had gathered, piecing together the puzzle of the mole's identity. There was another name linked to the crew leader's hackers.

Janet, Tim, and James stood from the table shocked, gathering the evidence accidentally dropping documents and flash drives on the heavily waxed floor. In a hurry, they grabbed the documents and rushing back to the control room to gather everyone and expose the mole. Their minds raced with the shocking news. The mole's true identity had blind-sided them, shattering their expectancy. They knew that exposing the mole was of utmost importance, and they couldn't afford any slip-ups, because he had been with the team the entire time.

As they entered the control room, their teammates looked up, sensing the urgency and tension in the air. Janet took a deep breath, trying to regain her composure.

                                    JOY M PIERRE

She and the others had to proceed carefully, ensuring
that they had all the necessary evidence and a solid plan.
But as they approached the table where they had laid
out the evidence, disaster struck. In a rush, Janet accidentally bumped into the table, causing papers and flash
drives to scatter and fall to the floor. The room fell into
silence as everyone turned their attention to the mess
on the ground.

Frantically, Tim and James scrambled to help Janet
gather the scattered evidence. They couldn't afford to
leave a single piece behind, as each page held crucial
information that would expose the mole's true nature.
Janet's hands trembled as she picked up a flash drive
and noticed that it had cracked in the fall. Panic surged
through her, realizing that they might have just lost vital
evidence. But she refused to give up. She carefully examined the flash drive, hoping that it could still be salvaged.
The tension in the room was strong, as every passing
moment increased the risk of the discovery.

Finally, with all the evidence gathered, Janet took
a deep breath and addressed the team. Her voice was
steady, though her eyes betrayed the weight of the situation. "We had an accident, but we won't let it interfere.
We have enough evidence to expose the mole and dismantle the crew leader hackers' operation. We must stay
focused and work together. But we have a mole among
us," she declared, her words echoing in the room. "Their
actions have put us all at risk."

As the team absorbed the shocking news, a mix of

emotions washed over their faces with surprise, anger,
and determination. Their trust had been tested.

And then it happened…

# Chapter 7

The safe house's alarms blasted, signaling an intrusion, not allowing Janet to reveal the mole. The team members exchanged worried glances, realizing that the situation had taken an even more dangerous turn. They were no longer safe. Without hesitation, Janet switched into defense mode and activated the emergency protocols, ensuring that the safe house went into full lockdown. Steel doors slammed shut, barricading the team inside while cutting off any escape routes for anyone. The air was thick with tension as they prepared for a confrontation.

Suddenly, the sound of footsteps echoed through the hallways, growing louder with each passing moment. The team members prepared their weapons, their instincts sharpened by months of danger and uncertainty. They were prepared to defend their lives and their mission. As

the intruders broke the first line of defense, Janet shouted out orders, directing her team to take positions. The
control room became the command center, where Alex
and Tim used their exceptional hacking skills, monitored
the situation, and provided vital information to guide
their actions. The tension escalated as the enemies closed
in, their footsteps pounded like a war drum. It was a battle of bits of intelligence and skills. The team knew they
couldn't afford any missteps or hesitation.

The team recognized the need for a planned success.
They aimed for a defensive strategy for interruptions
rather than elimination, conserving their ammunition as
much as possible just in case the door broke down. But
just as Janet thought she had the perfect plan, the door
exploded, blowing it off the hinge. Janet's team open
fire, shots was carefully calculated, and aimed to disable
the intruders swiftly and professionally.

Janet's voice cut through the tense air, issuing clear
instructions to her team. They moved with practiced precision in the tight enclosed area. Tim, his fingers dancing
across the keyboard, providing real-time updates on the
intruders' movements, exploiting any vulnerabilities he
discovered in their approach. His swift actions allowed
the team to anticipate the enemy's maneuvers, giving
them a crucial edge in the battle. The team members
worked in unison, their movements fluid and coordinated. They engaged in strategic fallbacks and advances,
using the tight spaces of the area to their advantage.
Their training and experience pushed them forward, each
member relying on their unique skills and strengths to

                                JOY M PIERRE

contribute to the collective defense.

The intruder's persistence began to feel the pressure of the team's battle from outside the room, and their initial confidence decreased as the team's intended defense upset their progress. The sounds of grunts and shouts mingled with the echoing gunshots, creating a disorienting sound of battle. Janet, Alex, Tim, and James led by example, displaying unwavering determination and courage. Their shared experiences forged a bond among them, further strengthening their purpose to protect one another and their mission. Minutes stretched into eternity as the battle raged on. The team's focus remained firm, their determination to neutralize the threat never hesitated. Despite the adrenaline coursing through their veins, they maintained a level-headed approach, making split second decisions to outsmart their enemies. The tide began to turn. The intruders' numbers decreased, and their aggressiveness gave way to fear. The team's relentless defense had taken its toll, and their enemy's spirit faded. And then, as quickly as it began, the attack came to an end. The safe house fell silent once more, the only sound was the heavy breathing of the team members, and their hearts pounding in their chests. Janet cautiously surveyed the room, her eyes flickering with a mixture of exhaustion and relief. The team had successfully deterred the attack, conquering against all odds. But they knew the battle was far from over.

James approached Janet, his eyes filled with determination. The taste of vengeance lingered in the air, and they knew he had an opportunity to strike back at the crew leader, the mastermind behind the attack. "Janet," James began, his voice low but firm. "Wait until I catch him…just wait. I discovered something interesting. He spends a lot of time at a psychiatrist's office because he is a psychiatrist. It's his vulnerability, and we can use it to our advantage."

Janet's eyebrows wrinkled as she absorbed the information that he presented because she never told anyone about the photo she discover from the blueprint. That moment she realized the phot that said Leader was the psychiatrist. She understood the significance of exploiting him at his weakness, especially after the ambush they had just faced. It was a chance to turn the tables and expose him on his own turf. Janet's mind raced as she tried to comprehend how James had uncovered the connection or her connection to the crew leader. Doubt and suspicion clouded her thoughts, but she pushed them aside, focusing.

Taking a deep breath, Janet nodded at James. "You're right, James. We can use his own tactics against him. We need to invent a plan to expose him at his psychiatrist's office. It's risky, but it could be our best chance to tear apart his operation."

Janet's mind raced as doubt and suspicion crept in. She couldn't shake the feeling that something was wrong. How had James uncovered the connection to the crew leader? Was he truly a friend, or was there something more to his motivations? Her eyebrows crumpled as she tried to piece together the puzzle.

                    JOY M PIERRE

As she took a deep breath and nodded at James, uncertainty worried her. She needed to trust her instincts, but the lingering doubts clouded her judgment. The plan to expose the crew leader at his psychiatrist's office seemed risky, and the stakes were high. It was a chance to turn the tables, but Janet couldn't shake the feeling that there was more to this. She paused for a moment, her eyes fixed on James, searching for any signs of trickery. Despite her doubts, she knew she had to proceed cautiously. The crew leader's vulnerability had been revealed, and they couldn't afford to let this opportunity slip away. Janet pushed aside her doubts, hoping that James was truly on their side, and focused on the task at hand.

"We need to be careful," Janet said, her voice filled with a mix of determination and caution. "If there's even a hint of suspicion, we could jeopardize everything. We must guarantee that our plan is airtight and that we have the evidence to back it up."

She glanced at James, searching for reassurance in his eyes. It was a delicate balancing act, and their trust in each other would be crucial in navigating the dangerous path ahead. Janet had to push aside her doubts for now and rely on her instincts. The mission demanded their unwavering focus and unity. Together, they could uncover the truth and bring down the crew leader, no matter the cost. But deep down, Janet couldn't shake the nagging feeling that there were still secrets lurking in the shadows, waiting to be exposed. She hoped that her trust in James was not out-of-place, as the consequences of betrayal in their line of work could be terrible.

As they continued to formulate their plan, the suspense hung in the air, intensifying the gravity of the situation. The uncertainty fueled their determination to succeed, but Janet couldn't help but wonder if she was playing into a larger scheme, a web of manipulation that extended far beyond her immediate mission.

Days of careful planning followed after relocating to another safe house. They rehearsed their cover stories, crafted their personas, and analyzed the potential scenarios that could unfold during their undercover operation. By then, most of the team split up because Janet lost trust in the others. So Tim gained multiple roles on the side of Janet and James. He tirelessly gathered intelligence and set up surveillance equipment outside the office, ready to provide support at a moment's notice.

On the day of the operation, Janet and James stepped into the psychiatrist's office, their nerves tightly wound like coils of anticipation. The atmosphere seemed harmless, with soft lighting and soothing music playing in the background. They checked in at the reception desk, presenting themselves as new patients seeking therapy for personal issues. As they waited for their respective session, Janet and James discreetly observed the crew leader from a distance. Their eyes scanned for any signs of vulnerability or wrongdoing. They noticed his cool, calm and collected demeanor. It became evident that he was skilled at concealing his true nature, making their task even more challenging.

　　　　　　　　　　　　　　　　JOY M PIERRE

Finally, it was their turn to enter the inner office, where the crew leader, disguised as a psychiatrist, would dig into their minds. "Ring, ring," James' phone rang, and vibrated. Janet kept walking. As James answered the phone, his expression quickly changed, signaling urgency. He motioned for Janet to join him outside the office immediately. Sensing the seriousness in his demeanor, Janet followed him, stepping back into the hallway before the psychiatrist entered the room.

"What's going on, James?" she asked, concern imprinted on her face.

"It's an emergency," James replied, his voice tense. "Something urgent has come up, and we need to leave right away. I can't explain much now, but we have to go."

Janet nodded, trusting James's judgment. She knew their mission was important, but their safety and well-being took priority. Without hesitation, she followed him as they quickly made their way out of the building, leaving the dimly lit room and the disguised crew leader behind. Once they were outside and a safe distance away, James took a deep breath and explained the situation to Janet. It turned out that James had received a distress call from Tim that the crew leader saw him enter his psychiatrist's office with an unidentified woman and called for backup. Their safety was in jeopardy, and James felt obligated to react without delay.

"We need to regroup and most of all recruit a new team," James said, his voice determined. "We have to formulate a new plan as soon as possible."

Janet's heart pounded in her chest as the gravity of their situation sank in. The crew leader had suspected something was wrong, and James' cover had been compromised, but because Janet had on a disguise, the crew didn't realize who she was. Their carefully coordinated operation had unraveled, and they now found themselves in a dangerous position.

They rushed back to the meeting point, their minds racing with thoughts of the crew leader's potential actions. They knew they couldn't waste time. They needed a team that could devise a new plan to have more manpower.

So Janet and James scouted for their team. Janet reached back out to The Fixer, while James reached out to his secret society organization to find a new squad who were reliable and trustworthy, eliminating the possibility of any weak links that could jeopardize their new plan.

As they united with the new members of the team, tension filled the room. The atmosphere crackled with a mixture of concern and determination. They gathered around a large table, lit by a single dim light, casting weird shadows on their faces. James shared the information of the operation, emphasizing the need for caution and quick thinking. It was clear that the crew leader wouldn't hesitate to use any means necessary to protect his secrets and maintain control over his organization.

"We have to assume that the crew leader is mobilizing his forces," James said, his voice firm. "We need to stay one step ahead, anticipate his moves, and neutralize any and all threats, now that we have no moles."

The team exchanged glances to each other, and one of the team members said, "Why would you think any of us would be a mole."

"We don't this time," Janet said. "The last team we had, we had a mole. It was the security guard, the entire time. He knew our every step and it allowed him to become a treat. He's the reason we're in this in the first place."

In shock, the weight of the situation hung heavy in the air. Each member understood the risks involved, but they were committed to seeing the mission through to the end. Failure was not an option. They began brainstorming, analyzing the crew leader's strengths and weaknesses, and considering potential courses of action. The crew leader had proven himself to be sneaky and mysterious, but they knew he had vulnerabilities. Janet's mind raced as she contributed to the discussion, her thoughts fueled by a mix of anxiety and purpose. She knew that their success depended on their ability to adapt, to think on their feet, and to trust in their training and instincts. With every passing moment, the pressure grew thicker. They knew that the crew leader was likely mobilizing his network, setting traps, and tightening his grip on their mission. Time was running out, and they had to act swiftly and decisively.

Finally, a plan began to take shape; a bold move that would confront the crew leader head-on, exposing his true intentions and forcing him to make mistakes. They would turn the tables, using their knowledge of his network and resources to their advantage. As the team finalized their strategy, a sense of grim determination settled over them. They knew the risks involved, but they were prepared.

With their new plan in place, they braced themselves for the next phase of the operation. The gravity reached its peak as they prepared to confront the crew leader, knowing the fate of their mission, and the jeopardy of their lives. They took a collective breath, their eyes locked with a sturdy tenacity. It was time to step back into the darkness, to face the unknown. Stiffness enclosed them like a blanket as they ventured forth, ready to outsmart their enemies and bring the truth to light. The team spread, each member assuming their designated roles and preparing for the next phase of the operation. Janet's heart raced as she equipped herself with the necessary gear, her mind focused on how everything was about to happen by confronting the crew leader.

Janet's mind drifted with a daring idea as she witnessed the team's coordinated assault on the crew leader's stronghold. While she trusted in their abilities and the plan they had devised, a voice inside her urged her to pursue another path. One that could potentially catch the crew leader off guard and deliver a decisive blow. Janet's gaze fixed on the crew leader's psychiatrist's office. The very place where they had intended to expose him. A

                    JOY M PIERRE

surge of determination coursed through her veins, and she made a split second decision. She couldn't shake the feeling that this was her chance to strike directly at the heart of the crew leader.

Without a moment's hesitation, Janet discreetly swerved away from the team's set course, slipping away unnoticed in the confusion of the operation. She knew the risks involved in deviating from the plan, but she felt a sense of conviction that this unusual approach could yield significant results. Janet's hands trembled slightly as she reached the safe house parking lot, her mind still racing with the audacity of her decision. She hastily climbed into her car, her heart pounding with a mix of excitement and nervousness. As she turned the key in the ignition, the engine roared to life, and she accelerated onto the road.

Janet's car raced through the well-lit streets, and doubt crept into her mind as the weight of her actions pressed upon her. The knowledge that she was venturing into a dangerous territory intensified the adrenaline coursing through her veins. Just as hesitation threatened to overtake her, a voice broke through. Adrenaline, her trusted inner self, reminding her of the mission's significance and the importance of capturing the crew leader.

"Janet, stay focused," her inner voice urged, cutting through the chaos in her mind. "We can't afford to lose this opportunity. Remember why we're doing this."

The remainder of the crew leader's crimes, the lives

affected, and the truth waiting to be unveiled reignited her determination. Janet's grip tightened on the steering wheel as she pushed forward, her mind sharpened on the task at hand. As seconds pasted, she refused to let fear paralyze her. She was prepared to face the unknown, to confront the darkness lurking within the crew leader's operation and her files. Minutes turned into an eternity as Janet's car finally pulled up outside the crew leader's psychiatrist's office.

She parked hastily, her heart pounding in her chest. But as she stepped out of the car, a sinking feeling washed over her. Her eyes widened in disbelief as she noticed her deflated tire. The unsureness twisted into frustration as she realized she had a flat. Panic threatened to overwhelm her, urging her to turn back and reconsider her options. But the stubborn voice of her inner self resonated within her mind once more, reminding her of the significance of this moment.

Taking a deep breath, Janet fought against the mounting pressure and made a quick decision. She couldn't afford to waste time, nor could she let a flat tire deter her from completing her mission. With determination, she reached for her phone and dialed for roadside assistance, requesting immediate help. As she waited for assistance to arrive, Janet strengthened herself, reaffirming her commitment to the mission. She knew that every passing minute brought her closer to her encounter with the crew leader, and she couldn't let surprising obstacles derail her purpose.

     

Finally, the assistant arrived, swiftly changing the tire and giving Janet the means to continue her journey. As she approached the office, she carefully surveyed her surroundings, seeking any signs of alarm or suspicion. The soft lighting and soothing music played on, seemingly oblivious to the chaos unfolding elsewhere.

Janet knew that time was of the essence. So the day her and James visited the office, she reached into her pocket, retrieving a discreet listening device. And planted it inside the office under the couch before she left, hoping it captured any incriminating conversations or revealing information. Her next move was equally brave but necessary for her plan to succeed.

This time she decided to disguise herself as a maintenance worker, equipping herself with a male janitor's uniform she had gotten beforehand. With a cap pulled low over her eyes, a set of cleaning tools, and weapons. She blended seamlessly into the background, assuming the role of an ordinary staff member. Janet moved through the corridors with purpose, her heart pounding with a mixture of anticipation and concern. She knew that one wrong move could expose her true intentions and jeopardize not only her own safety but also her reason for being there.

Janet arrived at the entrance of the psychiatrist's office, her pulse quickening. With a deep breath, she pushed open the door, stepping inside the dimly lit room. The plush chairs and inviting couch were still arranged in the same positions.

Janet scanned the room, searching for any signs of things out of the ordinary. She knew that capturing him here, in his own domain, would be an essential key to her mission. Every instinct told her that the crew leader would let his guard down in this setting, unknowingly revealing critical information that could shatter his operation. Janet's heart raced as she took a seat, waiting for the crew leader to arrive ready to execute her daring plan to capture him within the walls of his own sanctuary.

# Chapter 8

J anet's heart pounded in her chest as she waited in the dimly lit office, anticipation increased with every passing second. The soft music continued to play, its soothing notes a blunt difference to the intensity of the moment. Suddenly, the door swung open, and the crew leader walked into the room. His eyes widened in surprise as they met Janet's determined gaze. Time seemed to freeze as they locked eyes, a silent battle of wills unfolding between them. Without hesitation, Janet sprang into action, her instincts taking over. She lunged forward, surprising the crew leader and knocking him off balance. They crashed onto the floor in a tangle of limbs.

She fought with all her strength, refusing to let him escape or regain control. The struggle intensified, and the room was filled with the sounds of their struggle. With a burst of energy, Janet managed to gain the upper hand, pinning the crew leader down.

She took a moment to catch her breath, her eyes burning with determination. "I've finally caught you."

"What do you mean, you finally caught me," he said with sarcasm.

"You've been portraying to be my psychiatrist and a criminal mastermind, how could you?" she said, her voice laced with conviction.

The crew leader's eyes flickered with a mixture of anger and desperation as he realized that this was the reason for her fighting with him, in the first place. Janet swiftly retrieved a pair of handcuffs from her back pocket, securing the crew leader's hands behind his back. She knew that time was ticking, and couldn't afford any further delays. His voice trembled as he tried to speak, attempting to make sense of the situation.

"I don't know what you're talking about," he stumbled. "This must be a mistake. I've known you for years, Janet. I could understand if you mixed up me and my twin brother."

Janet looked deep into his soul, "What twin brother? You never told me you had a twin," biting her bottom lip.

"You never asked, he shouted followed by a pause.

                                    JOY M PIERRE

Janet's heart raced with a mix of emotions. Confusion filled the room twisting it into uncertainty. She had anticipated confrontation, but she hadn't expected a surprise. Could it be possible that the psychiatrist was innocent, mistaken for his twin brother? Her mind raced, considering the possibilities. She had to be cautious, not to let her guard down too quickly. It was crucial to verify the psychiatrist's claims before making any quick decisions.

With a firm grip on the situation, Janet spoke with a slow tone. "I am going to leave you handcuffed until I can figure things out to see if what you're saying is true." Janet's mind churned with conflicting thoughts as she weighed her options. The suspense hung heavy in the room, the air charged with tension. She knew that she couldn't afford to let her emotions cloud her judgment, but doubts crept into her mind. As she contemplated her next move, Janet reached for her phone and dialed James's number. She needed his input and perspective to help her navigate through the mess of doubts. The call connected, and James' voice came through, a mix of worry and willpower.

"Janet, what's up? Where you at?" James asked. "Is everything under control?"

Janet took a deep breath, trying to steady her racing thoughts. "James, I've captured the psychiatrist, but he claims to have a twin brother. I need your help because he claims he is not the crew leader and I don't believe him." There was a moment of silence on the other end of the line, the tension thickening. Finally, James spoke, his voice steady but filled with caution.

"We can't take any chances, Janet. We need proof before making any decisions. Look for any evidence that can link him to having a twin brother. We can't let our emotions cloud our judgment."

Janet nodded, even though James couldn't see her. His words grounded her, reminding her of the importance of following the correct path. She released a sigh and disconnected the call, returning her focus to the task at hand.

With measured steps, Janet began to search the office, her eyes scanning for any signs or hints that could validate the psychiatrist's claim. She precisely combed through files, photographs, and personal belongings, desperately seeking a breakthrough.

And then, she found it.

Tucked away in a locked drawer, Janet discovered a hidden compartment. Inside lay a collection of photographs, a family portrait that depicted the psychiatrist standing beside a man who was his mirror image, unmistakably his twin brother. The tension broke like a dam, flooding Janet's mind with a mixture of relief and realization. Her heart pounded with a renewed sense of purpose. She had stumbled upon the truth. The psychiatrist did indeed have a twin brother.

Janet swiftly turned to her restrained psychiatrist, her voice firm but filled with empathy. "I've found evidence. It seems you've been caught up in this web of mistaken identities."

The psychiatrist's eyes widened in distress. Janet proceeded to release him from the handcuffs, offering an apology for the confusion and pain she had caused. Right when the psychiatrist's handcuffs were released he picked up a desk ornament and smacked Janet in the face knocking her unconscious.

Janet's eyes fluttered open, her head throbbing from the impact. The room spun as she struggled to regain her senses as they were slowly coming back into focus. A surge of adrenaline jolted through her body as she realized she was now the one handcuffed. The doubt hung heavy in the air, a suffocating cloud of uncertainty. As her vision cleared, Janet's gaze fell upon the psychiatrist, who now stood alongside of his brother Charles, the crew leader as she sat strapped to a chair. The shock and disbelief registered on her face as she tried to make sense of the betrayal.

"What's going on? Were you a part of this the entire time?" Janet managed to moan, her voice strained.

Charles smirked, confused. "What are you talking about?"

"Did you really think it would be that easy, Janet?" the psychiatrist teased, his voice dripping with cruelty.

"You should've minded your own business. But this is most definitely like you."

Janet's heart pounded in her chest, a mix of fear and determination surging through her veins. She refused to give in to the misery that threatened to consume her. She scanned the room for any possible means of escape, her mind racing to devise a plan. But before she could react, the psychiatrist raised the desk ornament once again; the spark of wickedness in his eyes. Time seemed to slow down as the uncertainty reached its peak, Janet bracing herself for another blow. But just as the psychiatrist swung the object toward her, Charles kicked Janet's chair pushing it back, watching it tip in slow motion but not falling to the ground as he went to peek out the window.

Janet's heart raced thinking the chair was falling to the ground. The noise from the office commotion sent waves of panic rippling through the waiting area. She knew she had to act fast, taking advantage of the chaos that consumed the room. Janet tried to break loose the handcuffs wishing she had a spare key. Her heart raced with a mix of confusion and hope as Charles intervened, preventing the psychiatrist from delivering the final blow.

The unsureness that had gripped the room shifted once again, morphing into a tense standoff between the two brothers. Janet's mind raced to process the unexpected turn of events. Charles' eyes burned with determination as he locked his gaze on the psychiatrist. His voice cut through the air, filled with an intensity that demanded attention. "We don't have time for this. And plus I came here for my daily session. Let her go."

Janet's heart pounded in her chest as she watched the tense standoff between the brothers. She could feel the weight of the truth about to be revealed.

Charles' words echoed through the room, capturing their attention. The psychiatrist's face twisted with a mixture of anger and fear. He attempted to regain control of the situation, but Charles stood firm. The two brothers locked eyes, each aware of the situation and the consequences that awaited them. With a calculated calmness, Charles continued, his voice low but powerful.

"Man…I have somewhere to be in an hour, how long is this session going to take?"

The psychiatrist's face paled, and beads of sweat formed on his forehead. Just as he opened his mouth, a loud crash came from outside the office. And then a loud noise hit the door, "Boom!"

Janet's heart sank as she realized the door didn't burst open, thinking her rescue came to an end. Charles and the psychiatrist exchanged a quick glance. Janet's mind raced, trying to make sense of the Charles' actions. She watched as he continued his mysterious communication by the window, seemingly expecting a response, but not from the psychiatrist. Janet shifted her gaze to the psychiatrist, hoping for some clarity or indication of understanding.

To her surprise, the psychiatrist's eyes widened with recognition as he observed his brother's gestures. Janet's heart pounded even faster, a mix of anticipation, confusion, and a new layer of doubt. Her eyes darted around the room, searching for any signs of another presence. As tension thickened, she strained to hear any faint sound or detect any movement that could confirm her suspicions. Just as doubt began to creep into her mind, a delicate shift in the atmosphere caught her attention again. The psychiatrist grabbed Janet from the chair and rushed her to the bookshelf while the loud noise was going on in the waiting room, and Charles was standing at the window not paying attention. The psychiatrist secretly reached out, gripping the edges of the bookshelf and with a sudden push, it swung open, revealing a hidden passage. He quietly shoved Janet in and closed the door behind them leaving Charles behind.

Meanwhile, James and Tim burst into the office, their expressions a mix of worry and determination. Their eyes immediately fell upon Charles, who stood there confused and clueless. The suspense in the room reached its peak as they approached him, demanding answers thinking he was the psychiatrist.

"Where's Janet?" James barked, his voice filled with urgency.

Charles, caught off guard, stuttering, "I... I don't know. We were just talking, and then she left. I have no idea where she went."

Tim's frustration grew, his eyes narrowing in suspicion as if the walls themselves held secrets waiting to be unraveled.

"You must know something!" Tim exclaimed, his voice tinged with impatience. "She was in this office with you. Did she mention anything? Did she give any indication of where she might be headed?"

Charles' face paled, his gaze shifting nervously between James and Tim.

"I swear, I have no idea. We were just talking about... about our childhood, and then she said she had to go. That's all I know," he insisted, his voice filled with genuine confusion.

The unanswered questions hung in the air like an invisible fog. James and Tim exchanged a glance, their determination unyielding. They knew they had to find Janet, no matter who stood in their way.

The receptionist rushed in..."What are you doing to the psychiatrist's brother?" she yelled. "I'm calling the police."

James and Tim glanced again at one another, speechless.

With a firm nod, James turned to Charles. "Stay here. We'll find her, but if we discover that you're involved in any way, we'll be back."

By then Tim was completely lost because James didn't mention that the psychiatrist potentially had a twin brother. Charles' eyes widened in genuine shock and fear, understanding the gravity of the situation.

He nodded, his voice trembling as he replied, "I swear, I have nothing to do with this."

As James and Tim rushed out of the office, their footsteps fading into the distance, Charles was left alone with the receptionist, as she repeatedly yelled, "Involved in what…Involved in…?"

And in the hidden passage, Janet and the psychiatrist pressed forward, they ventured deeper into the concealed hallway, intensity hung in the air like a thick vapor. The only light came from occasional flickering torches mounted on the harsh walls, casting creepy shadows that danced and squirmed with every step.

Janet's heart raced, she thought they had stumbled upon a hidden world, an underground network operating beneath the surface, not realizing what she entered. They encountered obstacles, booby traps, and hidden guards that guarded the secrets she wanted. The psychiatrist's knowledge became their lifeline, guiding them through the treacherous maze. As they neared the heart of the hidden network, surprise filled Janet's eyes. She was amazed as they stood before a massive, richly carved door, adorned with symbols that hinted at unbelievable power and ancient mysteries.

Janet's breath caught in her throat, her pulse pounding in her ears. With a surge of adrenaline, the psychiatrist pushed open the door, and the suspense shattered into a mixture of awe and exposure. Janet's eyes swept across the chamber of ancient artifacts, her heart sank even deeper. The realization hit her like a wave crashing upon the shore. The artifacts before her were the same ones that were shown on the news, stolen from the museum where James worked. The pieces of the puzzle fell into place, connecting the dots between the crew leader, and the psychiatrist. The disbelief gave way to a chilling understanding. Janet was right in the middle of a vast conspiracy that reached far beyond what she could have ever imagined. The artifacts were not just objects of historical significance, but tools of massive power, wanted by an Italian Secret Society. Janet's mind raced, trying to comprehend the greatness, but wrongness that lay before her. The confusion switched into a sense of admiration and wonder.

Janet's determination ignited once again, fueled by a mix of anger and bravery. She had to uncover the truth, not just for her own sake, but for the completion of the mission. Janet's eyes locked with the psychiatrist, seeking the truth in his stare. But instead of the understanding and shared determination she had hoped for, she saw a flicker of something else. It was a momentary hesitation, a hint of uncertainty that sent her trembling.

Janet had a weird feeling about it all. The pieces of the puzzle had aligned too perfectly, and now a seed of doubt had been planted in her mind. Could the psychiatrist really be the mastermind of the organization they were fighting against, and lied by telling her it was his twin brother? A wave of conflicting emotions washed over Janet, she suspected him until he mentioned he had a twin convincing her she had the wrong person. Her trust in the psychiatrist shattered like glass.

Janet's mind raced, torn between her instincts and the psychiatrist's claim. The suspense swirled around her, heightening her sense of unease. She had to make a choice, one that could tip the scales in either direction. With a deep breath, she protected herself, determined to uncover the truth.

"Wait…I thought you told me it was your brother who was involved in all this, but you seem to know a lot more than you should," Janet's voice firm yet laced with a bit of uncertainty. "Why should I believe you're not involved in all of this? And plus you hit me with the desk ornament earlier, what was that about?"

The psychiatrist's expression shifted, a flicker of something resembling desperation crossing his face. The confusion intensified, each passing moment amplifying the weight of his decision. Would he be able to offer concrete proof, or would his true nature be revealed?

With a mix of fear and determination, his voice tinged as he began to speak, his words slow and deliberate. He revealed complicated details about his life, his past, and the events that led to this very moment. He recounted his encounters with his twin brother, a dangerous man confused tangled in a web. He spoke of their childhood bond shattered by the brother's descent into darkness.

The tension diminished and flowed as Janet listened, her mind racing to discern truth from dishonesty. She inspected every word, searching for inconsistencies or hints of manipulation. The weight of her decision pressed upon her, the fate of the mission dangling at her fingertips.

But even as the psychiatrist's tale unfolded, doubts lingered in the back of Janet's mind. The uncertainty clung to her like a shadow, whispering of hidden agendas and carefully constructed stories. She couldn't shake off the feeling that there was more to the story, secrets left unsaid, lurking in the depths of his words. With a heavy sigh, Janet made her choice. She couldn't afford to let her guard down, not when so much was at stake. The suspense transformed into a firm determination, fueling to uncover the truth once and for all.

"I'm sorry, but I can't take your word," Janet said, her voice tinged with regret. "There are still too many unanswered questions, too many doubts. Until I have concrete evidence, I cannot trust you completely."

The psychiatrist's face fell, disappointment and frustration etched across his features. The suspense settled into a palpable tension, the fragile trust he wanted to gather from her shattered. Janet knew that the path ahead would be filled with even greater challenges, but she remained focused on her pursuit of the truth.

As the hesitation hung heavy in the air, the psychiatrist's shoulders slumped, and he seemed to deflate under the weight of Janet's doubt. But instead of protesting or becoming defensive, he took a deep breath, his eyes locking with Janet's in a display of honesty.

"I understand your skepticism, Janet," the psychiatrist began, his voice laced with a mix of regret. "I cannot provide you with real evidence at this moment, but I can offer you my complete honesty. The truth is complex, and it's difficult for me to reveal it all in one sitting. But if you're willing to hear me out, I will do my best to explain."

Janet's heart raced as she considered his words.

"Try me," she said with a tinge of eagerness.

The suspicion surrounded them in the room, replaced by a hesitant curiosity. She couldn't deny that there were still lingering doubts, but she also recognized that dismissing his claims without giving him a chance would be a disservice to their mission. With caution etched on her face, Janet nodded, signaling her willingness to listen. She knew that the psychiatrist's explanation held valuable information.

The psychiatrist took a step closer, his eyes sincere and filled with a mix of remorse.

"My twin brother Charles suffered from severe psychological issues for years," he confessed, his voice tinged with sadness. "He came to my office for daily sessions, seeking balance and stability. I had no idea he knew about my private organization involvement with until recently. I deceived him, manipulated our bond, and used our connection to further my own agenda."

Janet's mind spun, struggling with the implications of his words and a newfound sense of understanding. She had suspected the psychiatrist, but now, a different picture began to emerge. The weight of her doubts shifted, replaced by a sense of empathy for the man standing before her.

"But why didn't you say a word? Why keep all this a secret? You've been tricking your brother, using him as a scapegoat. Dishonest about my records, making me out to be a person I'm not. Oh and sending others after James." Janet's voice trembled with a mix of frustration and confusion.

"James who," the psychiatrist demanded an answer.

Janet stared intentionally, "You know exactly who James is. James from the Museum."

"Wait, what do you know about James? How do you know him? He is a no-good lying piece of...Don't believe anything he has to say."

"Why not well let's work together," Janet said,

her voice firm.

"If James is your partner there is no way I'm working with you. He never pulls through with the plan and he always comes up with excuses. And if I see him again it won't be pretty, looking at her as a threat."

Janet knew he was the liar and she sprang to her feet, using her agility and training to swiftly dodge the psychiatrist's attack. The thrilling battle between Janet and the psychiatrist reached its peak as they engaged in a deadly dance of evasion and attack. The room became a battleground, filled with tension and the sound of their movements echoing through the air. Janet's determination to uncover the truth and the psychiatrist's desperation to maintain his secrets fueled their clash.

With each quick dodge and intended strike, Janet felt a surge of adrenaline coursing through her veins. Pushed her to her limits, she relied on her instincts and training to outmaneuver him. She stayed one step ahead, for her own safety. Their movements mirrored one another, and their bodies moving with sync as if they shared similar skills. The pressure intensified as they weaved around the room, their eyes locked in a fierce battle of wills. Janet's mind raced, analyzing the psychiatrist's patterns, searching for a weakness. As they continued their intense duel, Janet's frustration and determination boiled over. She couldn't let him escape or manipulate her, James, and poor Charles any longer. The atmosphere transformed into a solid insistence, fueling her every action. She had to bring him down.

In a sudden burst of speed, the psychiatrist launched a powerful strike toward Janet, and her training kicked in. She reacted swiftly, dodging the attack by inches. With a surge of adrenaline, she retaliated with a series of rapid strikes, driving him back.

The strain of the situation hung heavy in the air as the psychiatrist fought to regain control, his desperation becoming more apparent with each move. But Janet remained steadfast, her determination unyielding. She refused to be a ragdoll in his game any longer. As their conflict intensified, the room seemed to shrink around them. Janet's instincts kept her focused, her mind sharp despite the increasing chaos. She refused to let fear or doubt cloud her judgment. Their dance continued each move designed to disarm and offset the psychiatrist.

As the battle continued the psychiatrist's desperation grew with each unsuccessful strike, fueling his aggression. But Janet's persistence only strengthened. She refused to let him win, to allow his deceit and manipulation to succeed. Every punch, kick, and block carried her determination to protect those she cared for. She fought not only for herself but for the innocent lives that had been endangered by the psychiatrist's trickery. In the heat of the battle, the room turned into a messy scene. Furniture was overturned, art was thrown to the ground, and broken glass littered the floor. The room seemed to shrink around them, the more she heard crashing furniture and shattering glass.

The psychiatrist, driven by his own desperate need to

take control, lashed out with renewed anger. He threw himself back into the fight, unleashing a burst of attacks in to pacify Janet. But she was ready, her reflexes perfected, holding her ground. With a swift, well-timed maneuver, Janet dodged the psychiatrist's strike and threw a blow of her own, delivering a powerful hit that sent him crashing to the floor. The room filled with a heavy silence.

Janet's heart skipped as she stood over him, her eyes blazing with a mix of exhaustion and triumph. The battle had taken its toll, but she had become champion of that round. She had refused to let the psychiatrist win. So she fought tooth and nail to protect those she held dear and her newfound discovery, Charles.

Janet took a step back, surveying the wreckage with a mix of satisfaction and fatigue. The battle was over, but the scars, both physical and emotional would serve as a constant reminder of the challenges she had faced with her once friend and therapist.

# Chapter 9

The high-pitched ring of the phone sliced through the tension filled air, breaking the silence that had enclosed James. With a quick swipe of his hand, he picked up the cell phone, his heart pounding in his chest, unaware of the phone number. Relief washed over him as he heard Janet's voice on the other end, her tone filled with exhaustion. She used the psychiatrist's landline to place the outgoing call.

"Janet! Where are you at? I've been worried sick about you, everything good," James shouted, a mix of concern and joy coloring his words. "Where are you? Are you safe? Answer me."

Janet's voice crackled with urgency. "James, listen carefully. I was in the psychiatrist's office and he had taken me through a secret passage behind the bookshelf, but things took a dark turn when he discovered that I knew you. Well, I actually told him that I knew you."

James' grip on the phone tightened, his mind racing to comprehend the severity of the situation. He knew Janet could have been severely hurt and never found. The confusion in her words forced him to brace himself for Janet's next words.

"He became hysterical, James," Janet continued, her voice tinged with a hint of fear. "He attacked me, and it went down. I had no choice but to fight back. It looks like a battlefield here. There's crashed furniture, and shattered glass everywhere."

The gravity of the situation weighed heavy upon James, his jaw clenched with determination. The suspense of their battle played out vividly in his mind, the image of Janet defending herself increasing his sense of protectiveness.

"Janet, this doesn't sound good, and I'm going to ask you one more time, Where are you? Are you back in his office," James asked, his voice laced with concern.

"I'm bruised and banged up a bit, but I stood my ground," Janet replied, her voice firm. "Never mind this. But you have to get here before anyone sees that I'm hurt, and I'm not sure where I am. But I do know if you can get back to his office and find a way to enter behind the bookshelf, you will find me. I think it's a straight shot."

                                    JOY M PIERRE

The dynamic pause that followed was filled with unspoken determination and shared strength of mind. James knew that they were up against a challenging enemy, but the fight within him burned stronger than ever.

"Okay, let me grab a few things," James said, his voice filled with conviction. "And don't worry, we'll find a way to expose him. I'm heading back that way now and stay close by the phone."

As they ended the call, the doubt lingered, intertwining with their shared purpose. James' mind raced, adrenaline pumping through his veins. They were in a race against time, navigating a double-crossing path of secrecy and danger. But their spirits were solid, fueled by their unbreakable bond and unshakable beliefs.

James was in a rush to get to Janet because he didn't want the psychiatrist to wake up, or anyone else to get there before he could rescue Janet. James made it back to the psychiatrist's office to an empty waiting room, the office closed early from all the commotion. Walking into the office, James looked around searching for the hidden passage to get to Janet. On the back wall was a switch, engraved with mosaic art. James pushed the door open, tripped over his foot, and fell in, stumbling. In a hurry, he turned and ran back into the room before the door closed to get a desk ornament to prevent the door from closing completely.

James started his journey. Along the way, he was interrupted by the sound of footsteps echoing down the dimly lit hallway. His heart pounded in his chest as the tension grew. He ducked into the shadows, his body tense and ready to spring into action if needed. Peering around the corner, he saw two figures approaching, both dressed in the distinctive attire of a guard's uniform.

His mind raced, trying to think of a way to avoid confrontation. He couldn't afford to waste any time; Janet's safety was at stake. In a split second decision, he quietly slipped into an open office nearby, hoping to find another way around the oncoming threat. The office was dimly lit, with only the moonlight seeping through the blinds and casting creepy shadows on the walls. Broken furniture and artwork indicated the chaos that had erupted during a fight, but there was no Janet. James was amazed to see multiple stolen art sitting before his eyes. This very room was the key to the museums burglary. While seconds passed James was stood froze, remembering the location where each piece of art was displayed in the museum.

As he moved stealthily through the office, the uncertainty hung thick in the air. He was very aware that every moment counted, that danger lurked around every corner. Each creak of the floorboards made his heart race even faster.

Suddenly, his strong hearing picked up voices approaching the room. He knew he had to act quickly. Spotting an open door nearby, he carefully pushed himself inside. But as he reached another level, another obstacle emerged. This room had only one way in and

                                    JOY M PIERRE

one way out. He waited for the footsteps to stop so he could run out the room and get back into the shadows of the hall.

All James could remember was Janet telling him that it was a straight shot to find her. And his determination was to do that. He sprinted toward the last door on the long dark, and dimly lit hallway, hoping to see Janet. Time was of the essence, and he hoped he wasn't too late.

In the meantime, Janet witnessed the psychiatrist groaning as he regained consciousness, he clutched his head, trying to clear the fog from his mind. The room around him was in disorder, and the shattered glass added to his confusion. He could vaguely recall the intense battle with Janet, but his memory was fragmented. On the other hand, Janet was limping out the door into the hall, blending into the shadows of darkness.

Anger surged within him as he realized that Janet had managed to slip away. He knew he couldn't let her get away; she held crucial information about his operations. Pulling himself together, he quickly radioed his team, ordering them to find Janet before she could interfere any further. He staggered to his feet, collecting his thoughts among the chaos in the office. His mind raced as he realized the gravity of the situation. He knew if Janet and James came together, the two of them would be a major threat, and he couldn't allow them to unravel everything he had worked so hard to achieve. With a determined smirk, the psychiatrist decided to take matters into his own hands.

The uncertainty mounted as he hurried through the darkened corridors, keeping a watchful eye on his surroundings. The adrenaline coursing through his veins fueled his urgency, and of course, he wanted to get even with Janet for the last blow that knocked him out.

Janet snuck into a room and closed herself inside a tall narrow cabinet, peeking through the perforated holes. She watched for any sign of James, hoping he would arrive in time to assist her, just in case her hideout was discovered. With her limited strength, she couldn't imagine enduring another round with the psychiatrist or any members of his team.

Finally, in the distance, she spotted a familiar figure moving cautiously toward her. Relief washed over her as James emerged from the shadows. Silently, he walked into the room Janet was in, not seeing her, leaving out. From the inside, Janet carefully tapped against the cabinet door frame loud enough to be noticeable for him to hear, but soft enough to minimize attention toward them. Her anxiety heightened as she realized James had failed to respond to the sound.

Janet's heart raced as she considered her options. She couldn't afford to stay hidden in the cabinet any longer. Determination drove her to take matters into her own hands. With a surge of adrenaline, she flung open the cabinet door, stepping onto the floor tiptoeing to the dimly lit hallway. Just as she stood, a figure turned the corner, it was one of the guards. The intense moment reached its peak as they locked eyes, both startled by the unexpected encounter. Without hesitation, Janet lunged forward, and the guard caught her arms, but Janet took her forehead and lodged it right between the both of his eyes, taking him out. She quickly wounded the guard watching him fall to the ground, making him incapable of raising an alarm. But as the pressure began to decrease, Janet's focus returned to finding James. She knew time was running out, and they needed to regroup and strategize. She moved fast through the tortuous paths, determined.

Meanwhile, James, unaware of Janet's escape from the cabinet, continued his search. Annoyance hung heavy in the air as he explored every nook and cranny, his senses heightened. He couldn't shake off the nagging feeling that Janet was nearby, that they were meant to face this danger together. Finally, their paths crossed in a dimly lit intersection. Janet, gasping for breath, caught sight of James and called out to him. The goosebumps faded as their eyes locked, a mixture of relief, love, and determination passing between them.

"Janet!" James shouted, rushing towards her. "Are you alright?"

"I'm fine," Janet replied, her voice tinged with both exhaustion and relief. "We need to figure out our next move. The psychiatrist is still on the loose, and there are more guards lurking. We have to be careful."

James clings to Janet using a tight grip, his heart still racing with worry. The uncertainty that gripped him earlier slowly gave way to a sense of unity. He knew they couldn't afford to waste any more time.

"You're right," James said, his voice firm. "We have to stay focused and stay one step ahead of them. I have a plan, but we need to find a secure place to talk, that's not out in the open."

Janet nodded, trusting James' instincts. They moved quickly through the underground facility, avoiding potential threats and taking precautionary measures to remain undetected. The nervousness returned in full force as they weaved through the routes, their senses sharp, alert to any signs of danger.

Finally, they made it back to the secluded room where Janet was hiding in the cabinet with multiple files to be away from prying eyes and ears. The tension in the air was intense as they both knew the stakes had never been higher. They needed to take revenge and bring down the psychiatrist, their tough enemy, and manipulator.

As they huddled together, Janet and James exchanged everything they had discovered so far. The puzzle pieces fell into place, revealing a disturbing picture of corruption and manipulation. The confusion shifted from mere danger to a deep sense of purpose as they realized the magnitude of their mission.

                    JOY M PIERRE

"We need to expose him," Janet said, her voice unwavering. "But to do that, we have to gather solid evidence. The psychiatrist might be powerful, but he's not
invincible."

James nodded, his eyes filled with determination. "I
Agree. We need to be smart and strategic. We'll work together and watch each other's backs. This ends tonight."

As they set their plan in motion, the expectancy in
the room was thrilling. Janet and James knew they had
to tread carefully, as one wrong move could jeopardize
everything they worked for. They couldn't afford to
underestimate their enemy, but they also couldn't let fear
paralyze them.

Janet's mind turned with thoughts of revenge, but
she didn't let anger control her emotions. She knew
it was important to stay focused and be precise in
her actions.

"We need to find any documents, recordings, or
anything that can prove his involvement in the crimes,"
James said, his voice low but solid. "If we can expose
him and reveal the truth, we'll take his power away which
should strip his authority leaving him untrustworthy
from all his clients by exposing the truth."

Janet nodded, her eyes sturdy and focused. They
divided their tasks, combing through the room, searching
for any hints of the psychiatrist's misdeeds. The intensity
grew as they worked, the minutes ticked by, knowing at

any moment, they could be discovered.

As they delved deeper into the hidden files and cabinets, they uncovered disturbing records of organized activities. There was evidence of blackmail, bribery, and manipulation leading to the psychiatrist's corruption. Janet's anger surged because she was one of his victims.

Amongst the chaos of scattered documents and hidden truths, Janet stumbled upon a file that sent shivers down her spine. It contained detailed plans for an operation that would have catastrophic consequences for innocent lives. They panicked realizing the urgency of stopping this operation before it was too late.

"We can't waste any more time," Janet whispered urgently to James. "This operation is set to happen soon. We can't let innocent people become victims of the evil plot."

James nodded, as they made their way back into the underground passages, carrying all the evidence to expose the psychiatrist for misconduct, performing multiple heists, and photos of stolen Art from the museum where James worked. The urgency to take on the entire organization was high, and they knew it couldn't be done alone.

Knowing there was a slim chance of gaining reception for James' cell phone, he held it high in the air searching to gain at least one bar to message the photos for insurance to a trusted partner Billy. Luckily, James' wish came true. He walked close to a window, his phone lit showing two bars. In amazement, he was able to send messages to Billy. As they exchanged messages, anticipation reached its highest as James shared the critical evidence that was gathered. James read the last message, which said, "The evidence was stored in a safe place and let's focus on taking him down."

The intense seconds transformed into minutes filled with purpose. As they reached a dimly lit chamber, Janet turned to James, a grave expression on her face. "Stay alert," she warned, softly. "We can't afford any trouble. The psychiatrist is sneaky, and his followers are ruthless." But James already knew who he was dealing with.

Suddenly, a bang echoed through the chamber, shattering the silence. Their stare intensified as they turned to investigate the source of the sound. There, lying on the ground, was a small tape recorder that slipped from Janet's pocket accidentally. Janet and James exchanged suspicious glances, looking at the recorder.

"What's this?" James asked, picking up the tape recorder and examining it. His heart pounded in his chest as he realized the potential significance of the recording. He wondered if Janet was hiding something or if it contained vital information, as he continued to stare at her.

"Well… I placed the recorder in the psychiatrist's office the last time we were there, hoping to catch something we could use to pin against him. The recorder only records when a voice is detected. I didn't tell you about it because everything was moving so fast."

Without hesitation, Janet snatched it from James' hand before he could press the play button, pressing it herself. The tape recorder crackled to life, releasing the haunting voice of the psychiatrist saying, "Send all documents and funds to the Wonder Estate instead of Charlie2," like he was communicating through a phone call, and yelling, "Just do it."

The words sent a chill down their spines, and the air quality tightened around them like a drawstring. Their face twisted with shock and disappointment, this was another piece to the puzzle that they were unaware of.

As they made their way deeper into the underground facility, following the trail of clues left behind by the guards, the seconds grew even more intense. Every shadow seemed to hold a hidden enemy, and every sound made their hearts race. But they didn't give in.

Minutes seemed to blur together as the semi lit halls, darkened. Seeing and hiding from the guards of the organization grew more frequent. But Janet and James knew at any moment one of the lookout guards would see them and attack. Still not bagging out, they walked shoulder to shoulder and hip to hip, jumping from wall to wall attempting not to blow their cover.

Eyes wide and pupils dilating Janet lowered herself to the floor, army crawling closer to see if it was the psychiatrist. James on the other hand, saw Janet and sprang into action too. He placed his back against the wall, shuffling his feet inch by inch closing in on the human figure. They were moving with unity. The closer they came, the better their view.

They finally found themselves face to face with the psychiatrist, cornered in a room filled with stolen goods. James could clearly see they belonged to the museum he worked for. The tension was deepened when the psychiatrist locked eyes with James.

"What a pleasant surprise, look at the minimum wage guard in here with the big dogs. I thought you blew up in the explosion from our last encounter, or maybe you're a cat with nine lives, ha ha, ha," the psychiatrist mumbled, a cruel smirk dancing on his lips with sarcasm, and slamming his fist against the palm of his hand. James took off, sprinting toward him.

# Chapter 10

James had a vision of running toward the psychiatrist knocking him to the ground, beating him. Snapping back to reality, he knew it wasn't time for that so he stood firm preparing himself mentally for the confrontation ahead. Speechless, the psychiatrist didn't say a word waiting for James' response.

Not forgetting their previous battle, James anticipated another one to happen soon. But this time, James wasn't letting him escape.  From their fight before, James never forgot the pain he endured when Henry didn't make it.

Henry held the key to a lot of information, especially for what happened to Samra. He was the only one who could testify because he was an accomplice. So James desperately wanted revenge, at all costs.

Janet heard footsteps approaching, she turned around surprised to see the psychiatrist's twin brother, Charles walking in. But this time he looked shocked to see Janet and James standing there along with his brother.

James knew from a story Janet told that Charles had always been a bystander, ignorant to the psychiatrist's dishonesty and manipulation. However, facing him now held a symbolic significance, a chance to confront the twisted web of lies that had entangled them all.

James ran toward the entrance. He clenched the doorframe, slamming the door. "Boom." Everyone turned, startled by the noise. James pushed a file cabinet, watching it fall blocking the door. He wanted to make sure no one entered or left because things were about to hit the fan. Confused, fear, and misunderstanding was written all over Charles' face, realizing something was out of the ordinary.

"What's going on," Charles whimpered to the psychiatrist. "Why are we locked in here?"

The psychiatrist sat down, feeling trapped knowing he didn't want Charles to be involved in his deceit.

As James faced Charles, memories of the past flooded his mind, including the painful incident involving his sister, Samra. He couldn't shake off the haunting image of her lying unconscious inside the gas station bathroom, left for dead after being followed and attacked by someone from the same organization he ran with.

"You need to understand the pain your brother caused," James said, his voice shaking with emotion to Charles. "My sister nearly lost her life because of him. She suffered, alone and defenseless, while he continued his twisted games without remorse. And I was thinking of inflicting the same pain on you so he can see how it feels."

Charles' eyes widened with shock and horror, finally grasping the consequences of his brother's deeds. He swallowed hard, realizing the weight of his cruel mannerism.

"I never knew... I never knew he was that cold," he stuttered, glossy-eyed, turning toward the psychiatrist, fist clinched to his side. "Man, what's wrong with you, you must have lost your mind."

The psychiatrist stood from his seat announcing a secret from the past. The room fell into complete silence as the psychiatrist exposed information.

"We're all related," the psychiatrist mumbled in a low tone.

The suspense thickened, and each person processed the shocking truth that was unveiled. James and Charles exchanged stunned glances, their minds reeling from the unexpected twist.

"You're saying what... we're related?" James asked, his voice barely above a whisper. "How can that be?"

The psychiatrist smirked, his eyes gleaming with a mix of satisfaction and hatred.

"Yep," he replied, his voice dripping with venom. "James you, Carrie, and Samra, have the same mother that my mother couldn't stand. It hurt her every time I asked to play with you when we were young. We all shared the same no-good low down, manipulating dad. So we're all connected by blood. A family torn apart by jealousy."

The weight of the revelation pressed upon them, intensifying the already charged atmosphere. Janet, who had been observing the scene, felt her anger boil over. She had witnessed the pain James had endured, and the thought that it was orchestrated by his so called brother enraged her.

"No more lies," Janet's voice cut through the tension. "You won't get away with this, you've mentioned lies after lies."

The psychiatrist laughed, a chilling sound that echoed in the room. "Shut up Janet, you think you can stop me? You're all just ragdolls in my grand design. I control the storyline, and there's nothing you can do to change that. It's a family matter and I'm the oldest," pointing in the direction of James and Charles.

They all shared a silent understanding. They knew that the only way to bring down the psychiatrist was to unite, despite their complicated family ties, and unravel his carefully crafted web of lies.

As the psychiatrist's words echoed in the room, Charles' face contorted with a mix of anger and betrayal. He couldn't believe that his own brother had been behind all the pain and suffering he had endured growing up, wishing he had other siblings.

"You're lying! You had me believing you were the only one I had and this was the reason you treated me so bad," Charles shouted, his voice cracking with emotion. "How could you do this to your own flesh and blood?"

The psychiatrist's smirk widened as he celebrated in the chaos he had created. "Oh, but it's all true. I enjoyed watching you suffer, always feeling inferior to me, and always in my shadow. It fueled my power and control over you."

Anxiety shifted as Charles shocked them all, lunging at the psychiatrist, driven by a surge of anger and hurt. The room erupted into a brawl as they struggled with each other, knocking each other into the walls and falling onto the ground. Janet and James watched in surprise, torn between stopping the fight and letting Charles unleash his pent-up fury.

"No, don't!" Janet begged, trying to intervene, but James held her back, knowing that this confrontation had been a long time coming. Charles needed to face the truth and confront his brother's wickedness. As they fought, painful memories resurfaced for James.

He remembered the torment he endured as a child, the constant comparisons to an older brother, he never met and the loneliness that followed. It was a vicious cycle of guidance, and now the story was adding up.

Finally, Charles managed to overpower the psychiatrist, pinning him unto the ground. He stared into his brother's eyes, his voice shaking with emotion. "You were supposed to protect us, not hurt us. And we were supposed to look up to you!"

The psychiatrist laughed coldly, a creepy sparkle in his eyes. "And what are you going to do about it, little brother?"

As Charles' anger reached its peak, he couldn't contain his rage any longer. With a surge of pent-up emotions, he grabbed the psychiatrist by the collar, pulling him close. The room seemed to spin as Charles' grip tightened, his face contorted with a mix of anger, betrayal, and nervousness. In a moment of pure frustration, he released his hold on the psychiatrist's collar, and with a loud yell, he forcefully slammed the psychiatrist's head onto the hard cement. The impact vibrated through the room, echoing like a thunderclap.

The psychiatrist's world spun into a dizzying blur. Stars danced before his eyes, flashing and twinkling in a chaotic dance. He groaned in pain, his head throbbing as he struggled to regain his normalcy. Blood seeped from the back of his head, and the room fell silent, waiting for him to drop dead. The tension thickened as everyone processed the consequences of that forceful act. It was a moment of raw brutality, a testament to Charles' pent-up anger and desire for fairness.

Janet's eyes widened with shock, torn between concern for the psychiatrist's well-being and understanding the magnitude of his crimes. She exchanged a quick glance with James, their unspoken agreement affirming Charles' actions as a reflection of the deep pain and betrayal he suffered.

As the stars slowly faded from the psychiatrist's vision, he found himself staring up at the ceiling, disoriented and humiliated. The impact had left him vulnerable, his masquerade of control shattered. In that moment, he began to comprehend the weight of his actions and the price he would pay for his manipulative schemes.

Charles, now standing over the psychiatrist, his fists still clenched, felt a mixture of satisfaction and sorrow. It wasn't a proud moment for him, but it was necessary, an act that allowed him to release everything, and to confront the monster that his own blood had become.

James snatched the fallen psychiatrist from the ground and threw him into a chair. The grilling began.

"Why did you have our sister Samra chased and left for dead? James angrily spitted out. "What was the purpose?"

The psychiatrist whispered, "I knew she was my

sister, and I only wanted one of my guys to scare her, but you know Samra, she didn't let anyone pick on her without a fight."

James sighed, "Tell me about Henry," with mixed feelings.

"Who cares about Henry, he wasn't our family," shouted the psychiatrist. "He was only out for himself, and he was never your friend. And if he was he wouldn't have done things for me, to get at you."

"You threatened his family," James yelled with anger. "You know how he felt about his family and everything they have been through. He died protecting me, you know." James continued, "I worked under you for years and you never told me that you were a psychiatrist or my brother."

The psychiatrist smirked, a twisted smile forming on his face. "Ah, dear James, you were always so gullible," he snickered. "Yes, I played the role of a psychiatrist, but my true calling was far darker. I have fun manipulating the minds of others, tearing apart families, and exploiting their weaknesses, all because of how our dad treated us. And it was all a part of my organization."

James clenched his fists, his body trembling. "You used us, our vulnerabilities, our trust," he said through gritted teeth. "But why? Why go to such lengths to destroy lives?"

The psychiatrist's gaze turned emotionless, his voice empty of any remorse. "Power, James. Power and control," he replied. "I have fun feeling dominant, of having others dance to my tune. Our sister, Samra, was an ordinary ragdoll in my game. I wanted to see how far she would go to protect you and to test her loyalty to family members. But, because she was in a coma for three months, I didn't get a chance to make it that far. By the way, she did prove to be tougher than I expected. She's actually a beast."

James's anger consumed him. "I can see that you never cared about anyone but yourself," he said, his voice trembling with emotion. "And Henry... he sacrificed everything for me, for our friendship. How could you use him like that?"

The psychiatrist's face twisted into a sickening grin. "Friendship, and why are we talking about a dead man? Oh, James, James, James you were always so naive," he mocked. "Henry was nothing more than just a tool, a means to an end. I knew his weaknesses, and his love for his family, and I exploited it to my advantage. His death was merely collateral damage."

The room grew suffocating with pressure as the weight of the psychiatrist's deception settled upon them. James's mind raced with a mix of anger, grief, and a newfound determination to put a stop to their monstrous brother's madness.

James' eyes caught sight of a file on the psychiatrist's

desk. He quickly picked it up and skimmed through its contents. Within its pages, he discovered the vile truth behind the psychiatrist's actions.

"Janet," James shouted, his voice filled with disbelief. "You were right, he tampered with your files!"

Janet's eyes widened in shock that James was able to find another file and reveal the critical evidence. She snatched the file from his hands and quickly scanned the documents. Her heart sank as she realized the extent of the psychiatrist's manipulation. False accusations, fabricated reports, and twisted narratives portrayed her as a villain, tarnishing her reputation and credibility.

"Why?" Janet whispered, her voice laced with a mixture of anger and confusion to James. "Why would he go to such lengths to discredit me?"

James clenched his fists, his face etched with determination. "He wanted to undermine you," he replied. "By painting you as a scoundrel, he aimed to weaken the trust others had in you. It was all part of another sick game of his."

"I don't need you to speak for me, James," the psychiatrist yelled. "Where is your family Janet, and who do you have?" not allowing Janet to get a word in.

The psychiatrist's words echoed through the room, his voice dripping with disrespect. Janet's eyes narrowed, as she stared him down.

"You may have manipulated my files, but you can't erase the truth," Janet declared, her voice steady with determination. "I have my own family, my own support system. And I have the strength too..." as she lunged forward and threw a blow to the psychiatrist's nose. James grabbed Janet and pulled her back.

Charles, who had been observing the scene in silence, stepped forward, his voice laced with newfound confidence. "We may have come from a complicated situation, but that doesn't matter," his voice grew stronger with each word. "This won't tear us apart. The truth is coming out."

The psychiatrist's eyes narrowed, a dangerous spark in his gaze. He moves back a few steps, his mind racing to find a way to regain control of the situation. He knew that his carefully constructed cover-up was crumbling, and he needed to act quickly to save whatever power he had left.

In a sudden burst of desperation, the psychiatrist lunged toward his desk, his hand reaching for something hidden among the clutter. The room erupted with tension as everyone watched his movements, unsure of his intentions. But before the psychiatrist could grab whatever he sought, James reacted with lightning speed. He charged toward him, tackling him to the ground, their bodies crashing against the floor. During the struggle, fists flew and grunts of exertion filled the room.

Janet regained her composure and sprinted to assist James. She joined the fight, attempting to pry the psychiatrist's hand away from whatever weapon he had concealed.

Time seemed to slow down as the struggle intensified. The room became an infantry warfare. But then, a sharp sound shattered the silence, a gunshot. The room erupted into chaos as everyone froze, their eyes darting to the source of the noise. It took a moment for the realization to sink in. The bullet had missed its mark, which was for Janet but grazed the edge of the desk and embedded itself into the wall. The tension escalated even further, as everyone's survival instincts kicked in. They knew they were dealing with someone far more sinister than they anticipated.

Adrenaline coursed through their veins as they faced the danger that was about to happen. The gunshot had served as a jolting reminder of the stakes involved, propelling them deeper into the heart of the suspenseful confrontation.

Charles, James, and Janet exchanged determined glances with unspoken words. They knew that backing down was not an option. The psychiatrist, face down on the ground, his eyes filled with a mix of fury and desperation, scrambled to regain control of the situation again.

With a swift motion, the psychiatrist reached into his front pocket and pulled out a small rectangular object. A wicked grin spread across his face as he waved it like a weapon.

"Do you see this?" he mocked, his voice laced with hatred. "This is a little something I've created. One push and this room is caved in."

The room fell into a chilling silence, the gravity of the psychiatrist's threat paralyzed them, unsure if he was bluffing. If he pressed the trigger, their fight would have been for nothing. Their identities, their connections, and the truth they had fought so hard to uncover could be erased, leaving them ordinary puppets in the psychiatrist's twisted game, if it contained something explosive.

With a surge of courage, Janet lunged forward, determined to stop the psychiatrist from carrying out his wicked plan. James followed suit, his mind racing with strategies to soothe the threat. The room erupted into chaos once again as the struggle intensified. The psychiatrist fought back with all his might, while his thumb was on top of the detonator. The device slipped from his hands and slid across the floor. With Charles still frozen in shock, he was no help to Janet and James. As the struggle increased, a series of unexpected events unfolded to recover the device. Objects crashed to the floor, shattered glass echoed through the room, and the sound of grunts and cries filled the air. The suspense escalated, threatening to consume them all.

"Boom," the explosive went off with an ear-piercing blast, shaking the room and sending remains of debris flying in all directions. Janet, James, and Charles were caught in the shockwave, their bodies thrown against the walls, momentarily disoriented.

As the dust settled, they realized they were trapped. The blast had caused a section of the ceiling to collapse, blocking their exit. Panic surged within them, but they quickly fought to regain their composure.

Janet's voice trembled as she spoke, her words strained but firm. "We need to find another way out. We can't let the psychiatrist escape."

James nodded in agreement, his eyes scanning the damaged room for any possible escape routes. Charles, his face etched with determination, joined in the search, his mind racing to find a solution. Together, they explored every angle of the room, their hands and knees bruised and bloodied from crawling through debris. But no matter where they looked, they couldn't find a way out. The psychiatrist had disappeared without a trace, leaving them without a clear path to follow. Time ticked by, and frustration mixed with fear began to creep into their hearts. It seemed as though the psychiatrist had vanished into thin air, leaving them trapped in a dangerous predicament with no means of escape.

Janet's voice quivered as she spoke, the weight of the situation bearing down on her. "We can't give up. There has to be another way. We have to keep searching."

James' determination burned brightly in his eyes as he responded, "You're right, Janet. We're going to get him. We've come too far to let him slip through our fingers like this."

Hours passed, and exhaustion began to weigh heavily upon them. Their bodies were bruised and in pain, their spirits wavered, but they refused to give in. They knew that time was running out, and their window of opportunity was closing fast.

Suddenly, in the midst of their desperate exploration, a faint sound caught their attention. It was a delicate scraping noise, barely audible within the wreckage. They followed the sound, their hearts pounding with anticipation, and it led them to a partially concealed door at the far end of the room. Eagerly, they pushed the door open, revealing a narrow corridor bathed in dim lights. It was their only chance, their last hope of pursuing the psychiatrist. Without hesitation, they ventured into the unknown, their steps filled with a mixture of nervousness. The corridor stretched on, seemingly endless, but they kept moving forward.

As they journey deeper into the unknown, their hearts fluttered unaware if the psychiatrist was dead or alive. With the chase started, the hunt for the psychiatrist had taken on a new intensity. With drips of blood on the concrete in the same direction they traveled could reveal the truth that they were heading in the right direction. They knew their journey was far from over, but in that moment, they knew they had taken a significant step towards reclaiming their lives, their identities, and their shared humanity.

# Acknowledgments

In the journey of bringing this book to fruition, I am profoundly grateful for the unwavering support and love of the extraordinary individuals who have touched my life in profound ways.

**First and foremost to God,** I extend my heartfelt gratitude to the one who guides us all. I offer my deepest thank you for providing me with strength, inspiration, and purpose throughout this endeavor.

**To my beloved husband,** Gutemberg, your unwavering belief in me and your endless encouragement have been the pillars of my strength. You are my rock, my muse, and my partner in every sense. Thank you for being the driving force behind my pursuit of this dream.

**My incredible children,** you are my greatest joy and motivation. Your boundless curiosity, resilience, and love have not only enriched my life but have also shaped the very essence of this book. I am immensely proud to be your parent.

**To my family,** whose constant support and understanding have been a source of inspiration, I extend my deepest appreciation. Your love has always been my refuge, and your belief in me has propelled me forward.

**To my dearest friends,** both old and new, your unwavering faith in my abilities, countless conversations, and moments of shared laughter have carried me through the challenges of this writing journey. Thank you for being my cheerleaders and confidants.

**To "Push of Joy,"** my social media group of family and friends, I am grateful for allowing me to share my journey and for embracing my motivation during the process. Your enthusiasm and engagement have been a wellspring of inspiration.

This book is an expression of my art inspired by those mentioned above. Your love, support, and belief in me have been the wind beneath my wings. It is my hope that this book excites each of you like you've excited me in my life.

With heartfelt gratitude,

Author Joy M Pierre